Eric Delderfield's

SECOND BOOK OF
TRUE ANIMAL STORIES

Eric Delderfield's

SECOND BOOK OF
TRUE ANIMAL STORIES

I think I could turn and live with animals
                    they are so placid and self contained
I stand and look at them long and long,
They do not sweat and whine about their condition
They do not lie awake in the dark and weep for their sins.

Walt Whitman

David & Charles : Newton Abbot

ISBN 0 7153 5695 X

Set in 11-point Baskerville
and printed in Great Britain
by W J Holman Limited Dawlish
for David & Charles (Publishers) Limited
South Devon House Newton Abbot Devon

CONTENTS

LIST OF ILLUSTRATIONS

Photographs not otherwise acknowledged are from the
author's collection.

INTRODUCTION

My first book of animal stories was exceptionally well received, so here is another selection.

The world of animals is full of surprises. Many seem to know just what is expected of them, and their intelligence, instinct—call it what you will—sometimes leaves us astounded. The stories of Hamish, the dour little Scotch terrier with his 'down and out' pal; of the strange, comical and almost human behaviour of Charlie the crow; of Black's incredible journey across quite unknown country in search of his master —these are only a sample of the many tales that could be told about animal understanding. There are stories, too, which illustrate how animals can help humans, as for instance Japhet the pony and his spastic friends; Trixie the rodent officer on the council payroll; the trained sheepdogs. Included also are accounts of the fine work being done by people of many countries to alleviate the hardships of animals.

Let us not be over-sentimental. I have no more patience with those who let their animals rule their lives than with those who spoil children until they are a pest to all about them. These people do immense harm. Nevertheless, it must be remembered that dogs, cats, birds and other pets accomplish much in easing the loneliness of millions of people and in this way alone animals serve humanity in no small degree.

Finally, a sincere thank you to all who have helped me in

my quest for stories, though unfortunately it has been imposs-ible to include all the information that has been brought to my notice since the first volume was published. Whenever possible in using a story I have seen for myself, and in all other cases the greatest pains have been taken to ensure accuracy. In this connection may I say what a great pleasure it has been to meet so many nice people.

Acknowledgement for help given and for permission to use pictures appears elsewhere in these pages.

E.R.D.

Penshurst
Exmouth
Devon   1972

SENSE AND SENSIBILITY

A TOUCHING FRIENDSHIP

Quite remarkable is the story of the beginning, duration and ending of the strange and unusual friendship between a hen and a cat, at the home of Mrs Collier in the village of North Cadbury in Somerset.

There were two cats on the establishment. One had been a permanent member of the household for a long time. The other was a stray that just turned up. He was not accepted by the other cat and at first they quarrelled continually; but then, as animals so often do, they arrived at a compromise acceptable to both. The household pet reigned indoors, and the stray took up his vantage point on a window sill and slept in the conservatory, so that they rarely met.

This was the situation when one fine summer afternoon a hen arrived, and settled down on the window sill that the stray had claimed as his domain, helping herself to a drink of milk from his bowl. She was a fine glossy Rhode Island Red, well fed and in good condition. Later in the afternoon the tom cat returned and jumped up to his window sill. Strange to say, even at this first meeting the cat evinced no surprise, nor indeed did he seem in the least bit curious, unusual at any time for a cat.

Enquiries were made in the district, but no one seemed to

have lost a hen, so she just stayed on with the cat. The pair became inseparable companions, sharing the window sill during the day and sleeping quarters in the conservatory at night. The cat slept on a bed of hay; the hen perched on a shelf above: and they ate together from the same bowl, each giving way to the other in turn. Three weeks later the hen showed her appreciation by laying a large brown egg. This became a daily event and she always laid the egg in the same place.

So this strange pair settled into a pattern which never changed. Every day when the cat was groomed, then hen would fuss around until she too was brushed. That also became a daily routine. Meanwhile the other cat ignored them both. Two years passed in this tranquil fashion, until one day the cat was hit by a passing car, a fact that was only discovered when Mrs Collier went to give the pair their breakfast. Only the hen was there and eventually the cat was found lying on his bed of hay badly hurt. He was conscious and managed to lap up some cream, but he could not stand and his head was injured. The vet arrived but could do nothing except put him out of his misery. The hen stood by, watching every move intently, though she was taken out when the cat was put down. That evening the hen was in her usual place for a meal, which she had before going off into the conservatory for the night as usual. It was the last that anybody saw of her!

Naturally, the strange association of the two was known to the people in the village, and with their help a thorough search was made in fields, woods and gardens over a wide area, but the hen was never seen again and no report of any one having seen her ever came to hand.

Who knows, as Mrs Collier says, whether the hen is wandering, searching for the cat who shared her life so closely.

HENRY, QUINTIN AND THE FOX

Miss M. Price of Bexhill, on the Sussex coast, had a surprise when she found that the bread and milk she had put out for a pair of hedgehogs was being shared by a friendly fox. Bexhill, with a population of around 35,000, can scarcely be considered rural, yet Miss Price is continually being amazed at the way wild creatures call in on her.

The two hedgehogs were old friends. They dropped by one evening, were fed and thereafter made a nightly call for six months or more. Christened Henry and Quintin, each had distinct personalities and characteristics. Henry was a mild little fellow, but his friend could, if need be, become quite belligerent. One night while the two of them were enjoying the meal, a young fox sauntered up. He made no effort to hurt the hedgehogs and quickly joined in the meal, sharing the same bowl. It must have been superlatively good bread and milk, for he too began to make a nightly call. Just occasionally he so far neglected his manners as to try and exclude his fellow diners, but the more belligerent of the two promptly backed into him, his spine meeting the fox's nose, and emitted an odd hissing noise at the same time. Thereafter, the fox took the hint and behaved himself.

With the approach of winter the hedgehogs settled into the compost heap for their long sleep but the fox continued to come, and not without good reason, for, since the departure of the hedgehogs, his nightly repast consisted of breast of mutton.

One evening, looking out from her window, Miss Price was somewhat surprised to see a piece of lamb moving across the garden apparently under its own power. When she investigated, she found that it was in fact being dragged along by a tiny soft-bristled hedgehog. At that very moment the fox appeared. Realising that this was his own supper being whisked away, he grabbed the meat, shook off the hedgehog and calmly proceeded to eat his meal. Whether he would have shaken Quintin off with the same ease is a matter for conjecture.

When the seasons turned full circle, the original trio became a foursome, for one night the fox arrived with a beautiful, fluffy, greedy little cub which proceeded to bolt down all the bread and milk put down for the hedgehogs. But disregarding the bad manners of the newcomer the hedgehogs and fox continued to pay their nightly call, all three once more eating amicably together.

GIRL FALLS FOR BOY

Sultan, a handsome two-year-old alsatian, was in the habit of serenading his lady love in courtly and chivalrous style beneath her window in Avondale Road, Nottingham. She was Judy, a collie, and five years his senior. When and how they first met is not known, but Judy used to sit 'mooning' at the window waiting patiently for her handsome boy friend to pass by. Sultan for his part, as soon as he got to Judy's house, would sit down and howl.

One day when the family was out, Judy lost all sense of decorum. She had whined and wagged her tail in response, but her boy friend could not see or hear this, so he howled the louder. This went on for over an hour and at last Judy could withstand his amorous advances no longer. She opened the window clasp with her nose, pushed open the window—and jumped.

Alas, it was a 20ft drop and she landed heavily, breaking both front legs on the concrete path below. For some time she whimpered in agony and Sultan, very disturbed, barked loudly in sympathy. Neighbours hastened to the injured Judy, but the alsatian refused to leave her until she was safely ensconced in the People's Dispensary for Sick Animals.

At home Sultan could not be comforted and grieved all night. Eventually when the injured heroine, her forelegs in plaster casts, was taken home, the alsatian was taken to see her. At the sight of him Judy yelped with delight, and Sultan set about licking her devotedly from stem to stern. It was a delightful reunion.

Sultan is still on calling terms with the lady of his heart, and she has fully recovered from the day when she took the plunge for the handsome dog down the road.

CAN A DOG SYMPATHISE?

That animals, particularly dogs, have feeling and understanding is obvious to people who either own or study them. Even so, dog lovers are occasionally astounded by the degree of sensitivity shown by their pets, sometimes in the most unlikely circumstances. How often, for instance, does a dog in a car make apparent his like or dislike of another on the pavement, even when the car is travelling quite fast and one would have thought that there was no time for reactions!

Hamish was a dour Scotch terrier owned by Mr and Mrs R. F. Hartill of Nuneaton in Warwickshire. So jealously did he guard the premises that he would not allow either cat or dog to put a nose in the front gate. He would sit at the window for long periods, swaying slightly to and fro—and if a trespasser dared to invade he would go berserk, tearing out of the house with rugs and mats flying and skidding in his wake. They were rare and brave spirits who managed to stand their ground before such an onslaught.

The family were all the more surprised one day when Hamish was seen to be escorting a woebegone little mongrel up the drive and gently nosing him down to the doormat by the front door. It was all the more amazing because this was his own special holy of holies. Having settled the stranger on to the mat, he then went to recruit human help. This visitor was obviously a stray—dirty, cold, hungry and very, very scared. They took him in and bathed him, Hamish watching approvingly and adding an occasional lick of his own. The stray was then fed from Hamish's bowl and put for the night in Hamish's bed without the slightest protest from him. In due course the dog's owner was found, but Hamish was the courteous host right to the end.

How much perception and understanding? We shall never know, but it was all so out of character that only some deeply embedded instinct could have given rise to such impeccable behaviour.

Mr and Mrs J. W. Aldridge of Guildford (Surrey) also had a dog which seemed to be able to work things out in his own way. Not only was Pippin, a corgi, exceptionally intelligent but he seemed to delight in making himself useful. If any member of the family was ill, then Pippin became the messenger and carrier, transporting papers and anything else upstairs to the patient, a job he was prepared to do all day if necessary.

One of his great joys was to accompany his master, who suffered with arthritis, on his walks in the garden. One day on his perambulations, the master dropped his stick. He was unable to bend down to retrieve it but the corgi settled that. First he picked it up and held it towards the man. The corgi, however, was too short and when it was not taken from him, he immediately realised why. So up on his hind legs he stood and again proffered the stick which was then high enough to be grasped. Pippin again proved able to think out a new problem and find the right solution.

BLACK'S INCREDIBLE JOURNEY

One of the most famous and popular animal stories of all time was *The Incredible Journey*, Sheila Burnford's tale of how Bodger the bull terrier, Tao the Siamese cat, and Luath the labrador made their way across Canada. At the time of its publication it raised the age-old questions about how much animals know and by what mental processes they are able to undertake a journey which would baffle a human. The subject was again brought to mind by the report of a dog which

Page 17   Gimme that phone! (page 23)

Page 18   Watchman, what of the night?

recently undertook a journey across France to find its master.

Jean-Marie Valembois, a builder's foreman, whilst working at Béthune in northern France adopted a stray ten-months-old sheepdog, which immediately became very attached to his new master. Black, as he was known, rarely left his master's side in the next fourteen months. But then the firm that Valembois worked for, which was based at Marseille some 800 miles away, called him back to work at Châteaurenard, a small town twenty miles from Marseille. So the man decided to leave Black with his cousin at Béthune, thinking that after a few days the dog would forget him and soon settle down.

Within a few days, however, Black disappeared. He just left the house and did not return. Six months passed without news of the dog, until one day M Valembois heard that a black dog, distressed and dejected, was wandering about the streets of Châteaurenard. He scarcely gave the matter another thought, for after all Black had never been to the town before. Later, however, the dog sighted his old master. It trembled, made an attempt at wagging its tail, and then howled with joy. Exhausted, thin, and covered with mud, his search was over.

Doctor Mery, the leading French veterinary surgeon and animal expert, commented to a *Sunday Express* reporter, 'When a dog goes on a journey, it probably takes in certain visible and audible landmarks by which it might be able to find its way back. What is amazing about Black's case is that the dog traced his master to a place it had never seen before.' Those who belittle animal senses are once more confounded, for it would surely stretch credulity too far to say that Black's finding of his master was just pure chance.

COME-BY!

Complete harmony between man and dog can probably best be seen at sheepdog trials or exhibitions where the patience

B

of the master and the profound intelligence of the dogs are superbly co-ordinated. Some farms, particularly hill farms, would be quite impossible to run without the aid of the dogs, and most of them know their jobs instinctively. In all country areas, farmers and shepherds will readily talk, though usually with infinite modesty, of the quiet wit and forethought their dogs show in rounding up the erring sheep.

Mr and Mrs W. D. Reed of Duffields Farm, near Redbrook in Monmouthshire, are typical. Sheep farmers themselves, they became fascinated with the intelligence of the sheepdog and began breeding and training the border collie, not only for their own everyday use on the farm but also for competition trials and exhibitions.

In all they have seventeen dogs, the oldest of which is Sweep. There are also Jill, Liz, Dolly, Brock, Turk, Taché, Mo, and others, all deliberately given names that avoid the commonplace. Jess, another beauty, is dam of nine of the dogs, six of them still being trained. Just like human beings, each one varies in intelligence, character and personality. Some are often rebellious, especially in the earlier stages of their training; others are slow developers, and these, strangely enough, are often the best in the long run.

There is no telling how long it will take to train a collie up to the stage of competition work. A very few are in competition before they are twelve months old, while others take up to three years. The majority are born with a ready-made instinct to work sheep—even the town-born sheepdog has this if he is bred right—blood will always tell. They must be trained according to their temperament, in short, says Mr Reed, 'You treat them like kids, praise them when they have done well, and admonish them when they make mistakes'. In training young dogs, the use of the voice is the means of control. Even with first-class dogs things can go very wrong for no accountable reason, and if the master is not confident and a little bit on edge, there is no question but that the dogs know this, and it can easily put them off their stroke.

The training may take a long time and try the patience of both man and dog, but at last the day arrives when they are on the trial field together. The sheep are let out of the pen at the top of the course and the dog is sent to collect them, and to watch his skill in stalking his quarry and delivering the sheep back to his master is always a joy.

Some shepherds use a whistle, some the voice and at the international trials the dogs have to be able to hear for a distance of perhaps 1,000 yards.

On arrival back in the ring, the co-ordination of man and dog in the process of shedding, penning and singling is usually magnificent. It is a difficult job for humans, working in pairs or even threes, to separate two sheep from the flock; the dog does it better.

The eighteenth-century expression *quockerwodger* (meaning a hanger on to a coat tail) is an apt description of the dogs and sheep. We hear 'Come-by'—'Away to me'—'Away here'— or other familiar commands and watch the dogs react and obey. The trial ground is of course a far cry from the extensive mountain farms of Wales, Yorkshire, the Lake District and Scotland, where the dogs have to handle very large numbers of sheep, perhaps running into thousands. On such areas, it is estimated that they can cover up to forty or fifty miles in a day's work. But these smooth demonstrations with the sheep quickly penned or cut out, are examples of true expertise and give the bystander a glimpse of the difficult, complex work done by a sheepdog.

FOUR-LEGGED RODENT OFFICER

Trixie, a six-year-old crossbred alsatian collie, has a different mission in life—to kill rats. Her skill, verve, confidence and competence are such that she is employed by a local council and was even put on the salary list without so much as asking.

It all came about when one day she accompanied her master Mr L. Lawrence, chief rodent control officer to the Hatfield Rural District Council, on one of his routine expeditions to clear rats from a hedgerow. Trixie watched the operator go to work and then with an air of 'anything you can do, I can do better', she started a hunt of her own and immediately caught a rat. From then on Trixie would not be left at home and in no time at all became an expert. No matter how quick the rats were, Trixie was quicker, and by instinct she knew just where to bite her quarry. It was a quick, almost painless death for them. A short 'victory wag' with her tail, and she would be off again on another scent, repeating the performance.

The rat population in the area covered by the Hatfield RDC was increasing considerably, due, it is believed, to the campaign in the Midlands to clear that area of the scourge. The Midland rats moved south to increase the Hatfield population by 30 per cent, bringing hundreds of complaints from householders. In the neighbouring Hertford RDC, a dog died from leptospirosis, the killer disease carried by rats, which in fact had caused the death of two farmworkers in the Hitchin area a year or two earlier. Some twenty-five farms rely on the Council to keep the rodents in check, and the rodent officers have, of course, the normal run-of-the-mill assignments and work at the Council's own large refuse tip.

So Trixie began in earnest and was soon accounting for an astounding number of rats on her own. Mr Lawrence was amazed at the way she seemed to know where to look, and her methods of trapping the rats were quicker and far superior to the orthodox methods of traps and poison. Moreover, Trixie obviously enjoyed the job and seemed tireless: at the end of a long day she is still full of energy and ever ready for a romp with the children in the street. When it is time for bed she curls up on her own armchair in front of the fire.

Trixie's fame spread. On one occasion at the tip she disposed of fifteen rats in an hour—one every four minutes. Not bad going by anybody's reckoning. The Chief Public Health Inspector suggested that some record should be made of the dog's catch: it proved to be just under 200 in a year. As the descendants of one female rat can number well over 100 within the twelve-month period, Mr Bailey suggested that Trixie should be put on the Council payroll at £5 per annum, and it was unanimously agreed.

All this was two years ago and Trixie has not let up since. Of course, there are hazards in the job. Sometimes she is bitten on the nose by a cornered rat, but this is all in a day's work and she never gives up. Once a week Trixie calls at the office for her 'job card'. Here she is among friends and admirers and she has a wag of the tail for everyone.

Mr Lawrence, her owner, recalls how his wife brought Trixie home from the Blue Cross kennels when she was six months old. She quickly became a lovable pet and friend, and so she remains at home. But when there is work to be done— a-hunting she will go.

CLEOPATRA—PHONE FANATIC

Of course, it all depends on the outlook! Some people have a telephone installed because it is a necessity, a vital link with the outside world. To others it is just a convenience, and there are those who feel bound to have it but regard it as a curse, a noisy nuisance or an interfering menace (the author is in this last category).

At a house in Old Windsor, Berkshire, another attitude prevails. The strident burr is treated as a direct assault on the occupants of the house, from which they must be protected at all costs. So, every time the telephone rings there is a mad dash to hook the receiver off its rest. No wonder callers are somewhat disconcerted to hear growls and barks, and sometimes they are cut off altogether.

This is Cleopatra in action! Cleo is an eight-year-old Jack Russell terrier and has been a phone fanatic from puppyhood. Whenever the phone rings she dashes to it, lifts the receiver and carries it off to her basket nearby. Unless Mrs Nash her owner gets there first—and she is rarely quick enough—she is lucky if she can rescue the receiver in time to take the call.

All the family friends have complained of the cavalier treatment they receive on the phone, but when the boss wants to call Mr Nash urgently and cannot get through, it is no longer a laughing matter. So recently, after redecorating, the Nashes decided that perhaps a better place for the phone was on the wall, nicely out of Cleo's reach. The first few calls after that meant wild jumps to get at it, but Cleo is quick to learn; within twenty-four hours she realised there was a better way and she raced up the stairs to get at the second instrument in the bedroom. That is what she still does, though the humans now have a sporting chance of answering the phone first.

Cleo came to the Nash household when she was nine weeks old and is as bright as can be on many things. When the British Broadcasting Company heard about her antics, she was invited to appear on the television network. She behaved beautifully and showed to the cameras none of the antagonism that she has to the phone. She is a television enthusiast herself and will watch intently with scarcely a movement for an hour or more at a time. Football is her favourite viewing. When, however, the advertisements for dog foods appear, she hurls herself at the screen, whether for the food or at the dogs which usually take part no one can decide.

Cleo had a bad bout of illness recently and part of the treatment was the rationing of her drinking water to very small amounts at two-hourly intervals only. After the first day of pleading—and it was quite a heart-breaking experience for her mistress—Cleo worked out a possible solution. She simply went to the bathroom and sat under the shower, just hoping that someone would come in and turn it on.

The great Cleopatra of history captivated many by her charms. Cleopatra of Old Windsor also captivates people by her charms when they meet her, but not—certainly not—when she answers the telephone!

SHEA—A DOG OF MANY TALENTS

Shea is a champion Irish wolfhound. A handsome chap, weighing 12 stone, rising some 7ft when standing on his hind legs, and wheaten in colour, which is very unusual.

His achievements can be set out thus:
He is a champion of the show ring
Has had dozens of photos in newspapers
Has appeared on television
Appeared in a production of *Camelot*
Is equally happy as a watchdog or pet
And understands almost everything that is said to him
Quite a wolfhound!

His officially registered name is Champion Edgecroft Simon, and though he has won many laurels in the show world, he is to his mistress, Mrs Zena Andrews of Plymouth, still a pet and very much a member of the family. Shea came from Reigate in Surrey when he was seven weeks old, and that was four years ago.

By now he is an old hand at the show business, for he has appeared at shows all over the British Isles—at Glasgow and Manchester, Birmingham and Cheltenham, Peterborough and London. The travelling presents no difficulties, for Shea makes himself at home on the front seat of the car and from time to time, just to freshen up, puts his head out of the window.

His show successes are legion. To become a British champion of any breed, it is necessary to win three challenge certificates under three different judges at different championship shows throughout the country—not very easy. Twice he has appeared at Crufts and was a prizewinner on both occasions, but his greatest triumph in the show ring was at Manchester in 1971, where he was judged best hound of the 8,000 dogs in the show. He has also held the Irish Wolfhound Club Points trophy for two years in succession.

On one occasion Shea was appearing on the stage in a production of *Camelot* at a theatre in Plymouth, and on the Friday of the week's run, he had to be at the Bath show, 230 miles away. He left two of his pals, basset hounds, as stand-ins, and off he went. It was a hectic week but worth it, for he added 'Best Wolfhound' and 'Best Hound' to his laurels.

Naturally, wherever he goes he attracts a lot of attention, but he takes this in his stride—and his stride is enormous for his hind legs are 3ft long. His mistress, however, admits to getting tired of the remark made regularly by hundreds of people: 'I should put a saddle on him'. Strange though it may seem, they all think it original!

For an animal of this size and description he has a remarkably equable temperament and most of the endearing habits of an ordinary pet. He is exercised three or four times a day and loves to pretend he is on a hunt. Despite living by the sea, swimming is not one of his favourite pursuits, although he enjoys the sands. He is allowed to share his owner's bedroom, and will in no circumstances go to sleep before his nightly drink of milk. Mrs Andrews is quite honest about it all. 'If you think he owns us rather than the other way round, you would probably be right', she comments.

One of Shea's fancies is that he is very fierce. He tries his hardest to live up to the wolfhound's ancient motto, 'Fierce when provoked, gentle when stroked'. At night he will stand inside the shop premises and growl furiously, at the same time wagging his tail with such careless abandon that he sometimes injures it. On occasions his ancient instincts still assert themselves and he will with little effort catch a rabbit or a hare.

Shea is extremely intelligent, and when he appeared on a television programme knew by instinct that he must do all the right things. He did too, commencing with licking the interviewer as if he was the sole object of his affections.

Naturally many people have cast covetous eyes on Shea, among them several Americans. One, a rich young racehorse owner from Virginia, offered the princely sum of £2,000 ($5,200) for him. But Shea is not for sale. Of Irish ancestry he may be, but his home is Devon and it is going to stay that way.

Preparing for outings in which he is not to be included means communicating with the rest of the family in sign language. To mention the fact openly would mean that Shea would be in his accustomed front seat in one bound, for like most youngsters of this day and age he loves the car, and his size and weight give him every advantage in a tussle for a place. But he meets his match in eight-months-old Alice, another wolfhound and one of his companions. This youngster is thriving, and so she should be with a daily intake of 4lb of meat, 4 eggs, 3 pints of milk and $\frac{1}{2}$lb of biscuits.

The boss of them all, however, is Annie, a seven-year-old basset hound, who looks positively tiny beside Shea. But size is not everything and if she feels inclined Annie will muscle in where angels fear to tread, and take the food from under the wolfhounds' very noses.

DOG EARNED HIS DINNER

Mr J. Vowles who runs the sub-post office at Newton Row, Birmingham, England, has as his constant companion, for both social and security reasons, a handsome black alsatian with sable markings who rejoices in the official pedigree name of Aston Ritter. This is rather too much of a mouthful, so from an early age he has been known simply as Dog.

Dog is a well-adjusted animal, extremely fond of children,

and even though he is now nine years old ever ready for a game. But he knows to a nicety how many beans make five and does not confuse a game with the fierce tussle of life. That he can tell the difference between those who enter the shop to buy and those who come in with a more sinister purpose in mind was made quite clear one summer morning recently when he accompanied his master to the shop as usual.

Mr Vowles was on his own and Dog was reclining behind the counter. Suddenly two men burst into the shop demanding money. Dog came to life with a vengeance, leapt up snarling and was at the intruders like a shot. They turned tail and fled, with the alsatian on their heels, making for a get-away car parked outside. They drove off, a witness said, as if the devil was after them. The whole episode was over so quickly that Mr Vowles hardly saw the raiders. He did not know whether they had been bitten or not—but he was quite sure that on this particular day Dog really had earned his dinner.

BEN—A GOLF ENTHUSIAST

There is no end to the way animals make themselves useful, and they generally manage to enjoy themselves in the process. An unusual duty however, is the one carried out by Ben, a three year-old black labrador belonging to Rod Wiseman, a professional golfer at Aldershot in Hampshire.

Ever since Ben was eight weeks old he has accompanied his master to the golf club. In the course of time he noticed that whenever pupils were taken out for golf instruction, a small hold-all, full of balls, went too. After a while Ben took possession of the bag and assigned himself the duty of carrying it for the duration of the lessons. It was this eagerness to help which led to his next job.

A television picture of a French girl delivering newspapers from a small cart pulled by a dog gave Mr Wiseman the idea of making a golf trolley for Ben. He persuaded an engineer to design a light trolley and harness which Ben could pull. When first harnessed up, Ben was not at all sure about the idea and refused to move, but the usual offerings of chocolate soon persuaded him to make a start and he has seemed to enjoy it ever since. Just occasionally he loses his professional dignity by giving chase to a squirrel, but this is merely an interlude to establish his territory. Well-meaning busybodies complained to the local branch of the Royal Society for the Prevention of Cruelty to Animals, who sent an officer to see for himself, but after studying the trolley and examining Ben when he had finished a round, he expressed himself completely satisfied. Mr Wiseman estimates that in going round the course Ben probably covers seven or eight miles, but if he was running free would probably cover four times the distance.

Ben is a fit and happy dog with a wonderfully gentle temperament, and like most of the golfing fraternity he has learnt to look forward to the 19th hole, where he receives fresh meat and biscuits.

ROBERTSON LEARNT THE LESSON

Without doubt most cat owners deplore the predatory nature of their pets as far as birds are concerned. Often too, the presence of a cat means that its owner is deprived of bird life in the garden. Lady Dowding's way of overcoming the problem is both instructive and amusing.

Her stepson owned a cat which rejoiced in the name of Robertson, because, of course, he was a proud and beautiful *marmalade* cat (Robertson's marmalade being known in almost every British home). When his owner had to go to America on a protracted trip, Lady Dowding accepted guardianship for the period.

Soon a difficulty arose. The family loved the birds in the vicinity and so did Robertson, but for an entirely different reason. His hunting efforts were punished in a variety of ways without any real result, until someone hit on the idea of 'sending him to Coventry' the next time he caught a bird. Certainly his food was put down and he was let in and out, but no one in the household spoke to him or appeared to notice him. Gradually it seemed to dawn on Robertson that this was deliberate and he switched on all his feline charm. He tried jumping up on to their knees but still they affected not to notice him and moved elsewhere. He ran up the curtains and performed his whole repertoire of forbidden tricks until, convulsed with laughter, the family had to retire to another room.

This crash course lasted only twenty-four hours on two occasions when he caught a bird, and it cured him. Snapshots of Robertson basking beneath the bird table and the birds' complete lack of fear prove the point.

Lady Dowding's own cat never caught birds, but the treatmen was tried out on other cats and was found to work with them too. The theory is that the cat is such a proud creature that the very idea of being unnoticed is more than it can bear.

PEOPLE IN THE MASS—UGH!

Animals, like humans, have their likes and dislikes. More often than not, the animal takes decisive steps in the matter and refuses point blank to be a martyr! A fine male tabby cat owned by a family who have a very large caravan holiday park in Devonshire did just that.

He arrived when a kitten, as a present for the children, and soon settled into routine. In addition to the three children, there were two handsome alsatians. a brown one named Jasper, and the other black, called Jet. For a year the cat walked about the holiday park, as his fraternity do, poking his nose into everything. He had the run of the house and the farm buildings, and on occasions when the children were a bit too playful or possessive, would make off to the barn and get away from it all by going to sleep in the hay.

As Easter came round in his first year, he was surprised at the great influx of new people. By Whitsun, when the normal population had more than doubled, he found it unbearable and one could almost hear him saying, 'I am not standing for this another year'. Neither did he. When the human deluge commenced next Whitsun he, metaphorically speaking, packed his bag and left. He was away all the summer and no one saw a sign of him. He was written off as lost.

On the day of the first frost, the cat, sleek and well-fed, arrived home. From the children particularly he had a welcome like that of the prodigal son, and in true cat manner he lapped it up, accepted it as no more than his right and graciously consented to settle down for the autumn and winter, claiming as by right the best position in front of the fire.

The following year, he treated with disdain the arrival in mild numbers of touring vans and people for Easter, but on the Thursday of Whit week he just disappeared again. The family were resigned this time and told themselves he would be back. He was too—at the first frost.

For three years now he has followed the same timetable. No one knows where he goes but he certainly neither wants nor starves. When the holiday-park population drops and the air has a seasonal bite to it, they know that 'Johnny will come marching home again'.

Some people do not like cats. This is a cat that only likes some people, and even then in mild doses!

JAPHET—STILL A PERSONALITY

There are not many who discover a new way of serving others at the end of an extremely busy life and as old age creeps on. This, however, is the story of Japhet, a pony of mixed ancestry, descended from Arab and New Forest stock, and a real character if ever there was one.

In the period 1957-64, Japhet was the mainstay of the West Norfolk Pony Club team. In those eight years he helped to carry the team through to the finals on six occasions: they were second in 1962, and won in 1963 and 1964. He has been Members' Pony Club champion three times, in itself a record, and—ridden by Mrs Allhusen—he was twice champion of the Combined Dressage and Show Jumping title at Wembley. He shares his favours, however, and has been ridden by four of the five members of the Allhusen family.

This highly intelligent animal makes no secret of his love of the limelight and is a real show-off. It came as no surprise to his friends that he was chosen as one of the horse personalities at the Horse of the Year show at Wembley in 1964, and Japhet unashamedly and obviously adored being in the spotlight, and every minute of the applause.

But show business is behind him. At twenty-one Japhet is an old stager and instead of going out to grass for the rest of his days, his intelligence, discipline and know-how are being used in a first-class service for others.

Major Derek Allhusen, who was a member of Britain's Pentathlon team at the 1948 winter Olympics and who led Britain's team to a gold medal at Mexico in 1968, is chairman of the Norwich Branch of the Riding for the Disabled organisation. Assisted by his wife, he has won strong local support for their efforts, for he maintains that handicapped children have a natural affinity with animals and are more understanding than normally healthy and physically sound children.

So Japhet, among others, has been brought in to help and he seems to understand that he must take particular care of his charges, who range from ten to fifteen years of age and are very severely handicapped. Many are spastic and spina bifida cases from the Clare School for Handicapped Children in Norwich.

This branch of Riding for the Disabled was started at Norwich in 1968, but Major Allhusen makes it clear that they are by no means pioneers in this particular aspect of treatment of the handicapped. The outings for the children take place on Major Allhusen's farm in Norfolk and they are the high spots of the children's week. Mothers assist in groups of three to each child, one on each side and one leading the pony. The riding is an incredible help in strengthening the children's sense of balance and damaged spines, and the medical authorities are very enthusiastic about it. These young riders display a fine courage and some even go over small jumps.

MAGGIE MAY LIKES HER PINT!

There was once a Welsh pony who was put up for sale at Barnet Fair in Hertfordshire. Sold and repurchased, the mare in due course was in foal to an Appaloosa stallion and at this period was purchased by someone in Kent. A fine foal was born, and was named Maggie May.

Alas, very soon afterwards the mother was killed in a road accident and Maggie had to be reared by hand. Such a start in life did not make the foal robust. But lean and skinny though she was, she caught the eye of Mr Fred Chilmaid who had started a livery stables at Bean, near Dartford in Kent. He purchased her and she joined the rest of the contingent at the stables.

Maggie May soon showed a love for human company, especially that of children, and quickly established an attachment to Gillian, the nine-year-old daughter of the licensee of the local public house, the Royal Oak. And so it was that Maggie May was allowed into the bar one day when Mr Chilmaid called for a pint. Maggie was not only curious, but apparently envious as well, and she licked avidly a finger dipped in the beer and made obvious signs for more. So she acquired the taste and now, with her own tankard, she has her daily pint as a matter of course.

Maggie May is now two years old and beloved by all around. Mr Chilmaid has promised her to the daughter of another licensee at the Rising Sun in Northfleet, but will continue to stable her. So Maggie May will be able to keep up the invigorating custom of 'whetting her whistle'!

DONKEYS FROM BEHIND THE IRON CURTAIN

The patient, uncomplaining and good natured beast the donkey is to be found in most countries in the world. One of the most attractive breeds is that native to Bulgaria, where it is used largely in the tobacco industry for carrying the leaf down the mountains. Extremely sure footed and graceful, the Bulgarian donkeys are dark in colour, some of them completely black, and all lacking the creamy coloured muzzle and underparts that are a general characteristic of donkeys. They are very fast, have narrow heads and slender legs which belie their considerable strength. Above all, they are very intelligent.

It was for this reason that Lady Monica Sternberg, who has a donkey stud at Plurenden Manor, High Halden, Kent, went behind the Iron Curtain to obtain some of these donkeys and was successful in bringing thirteen of them back to England. Arack was the first Bulgarian foal to be born. He was very lively and soon enjoyed the distinction of appearing on a children's television programme. Arack was followed by a black filly, and soon Lady Sternberg hopes to cross them with the Irish and English donkeys at the stud, in an endeavour to breed a more robust and streamlined animal for children to ride.

There are more than eighty donkeys at Plurenden Manor, many of quite different types, all presumably deriving from

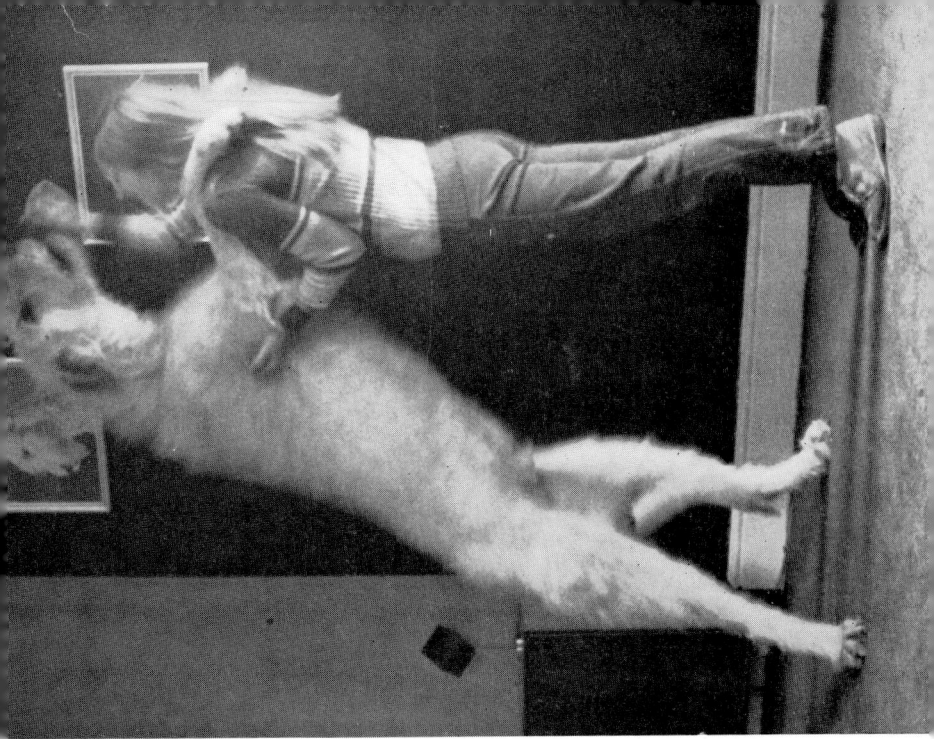

Page 35 (*above*) Shea poses with Alice (page 27); (*right*) Shea, the wolfhound, towers over his mistress (page 25)

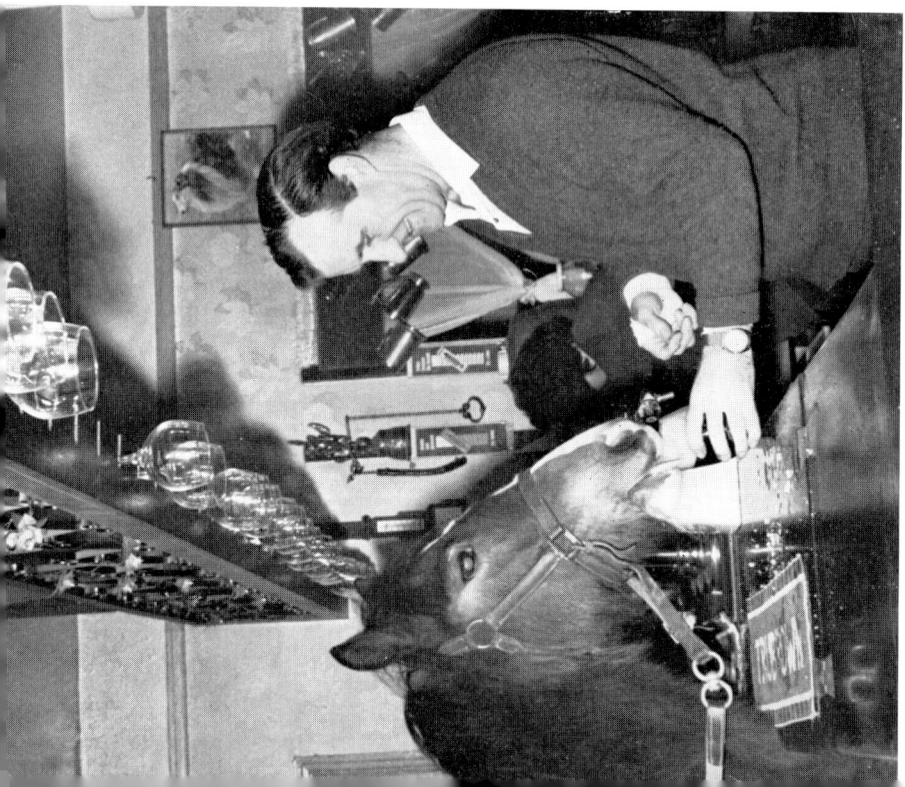

the various breeds of wild ass. Whilst perhaps the standard of intelligence may vary, there is one thing they have in common—an entire absence of stupidity. What a pity the same cannot be said of the human race!

Mr Cecil Newton, a fourth generation Romany who farms at Washingborough in Lincolnshire, also owns and breeds donkeys. Another interest of his is the breeding of Dexter cows, diminutive creatures that average 32-34in in height at the shoulder and weigh something in the region of 3cwt, compared with the 10-12cwt of ordinary cattle. Minnie, one of the smallest cows, is $3\frac{1}{2}$ years old and has had one calf. Ferocious Fred, one of the three bulls in the herd, can give Minnie and the other girls only an inch in height despite his name.

Mr Newton has heard on good authority that this type of cow was formerly bred to provide food in the old sailing ships. They took up a minimum of space in the ships until they were needed as meat for the voyagers.

A DONKEY SERENADES

Was Zooloo an intelligent donkey? She forgot her calling card and chose the wrong time to call anyway. Whether she took people 'for a ride' on her own initiative or whether someone took her for a ride as a prank has never been discovered, but the fact remains that at 2.30 one morning the occupants of an apartment house in Statten Island, New York City, were awakened to the braying of a donkey.

Mr Giovinazza had arrived home from a bowling alley around midnight and there was no sign of a donkey then. He went to bed and to sleep, but twice woke up hearing strange noises. Thinking he had been dreaming, it was not until he was awakened for the third time that he actually got up and looked into the hallway. He still thought he was dreaming,

c

for there looking at him and starting to mount the stairs was a 350lb donkey. Realising at last that this was a real live intruder, he telephoned the police, who decided it was a job for the American Society for the Prevention of Cruelty to Animals.

The officer on duty responded to the call but on arrival decided he needed help, so he called the ASPCA manager, Mr Hollinde. Meanwhile neighbours and volunteer helpers had forgathered and, like crowds the world over, were excelling themselves in giving free advice on how to coax Zooloo from the apartment house on to the street. For half an hour the two men from the ASPCA did all they knew to get the donkey to move. They pushed and pulled, they bribed with carrots, apples and bread, and finally they succeeded. The next problem was to get her into their van, but a prime specimen like Zooloo would not fit into the one they had brought, so a larger truck had to be sent for. Meanwhile the adventurer was tied to a fire hydrant.

The truck arrived and then they began pushing, pulling and bribing all over again. As dawn broke the donkey was successfully loaded, and for two days was housed at the Society's home enjoying meals of apples and grain, whilst they tried to find a home for her.

The story had a happy ending. At a donkey stables some two miles from Mr Giovinazza's apartment, the owner counting heads realised that one called Zooloo was missing. But the mystery of how she strayed two miles remains unsolved. Unless she went under her own power, it would have taken two hefty fellows to get her there, even had they used the encouragement the ASPCA found only partially effective, a bunch of carrots.

HAMBONE, THE LOVABLE MULE

The following newspaper announcement ended the amazing

story of Hambone, once a pack mule attached to the United
States Army:

> The US Army regrets to announce the death after a heart attack
> of No 5911 Hamilton T. Bone, the oldest of two army mules at
> Fort Carson, Colorado. He was thirty-nine.

All his life Hambone had been a celebrity. Not only during
his army service but in a variety of other capacities he had
gained the newspaper headlines. And he was a celebrity to
the very end, for he was given a military-style funeral, including the firing of a last salute for a mule beloved by all his
army colleagues and by a host of others, not least the children
who came to know him during his retirement.

The mule who was to be officially registered in the army
as Hamilton T. Bone No 5911, was born in Tennessee in
1932. From the first he was exceptional, for he had a silvery
white coat and an albino mule is a rarity. He grew into a fine
animal, leading a normal kind of life until 1942, when he was
purchased by the army at the rock-bottom price of 120 dollars and subsequently posted to the 4th Field Artillery to
serve as a pack mule.

He proved an ideal recruit, very quick on the uptake, and
soon learned how to hurry into the traces of a caisson and to
pull with all his great might. When the guns that he pulled
started firing their salvoes, he stood by steady and fearless.
Under such circumstances he was a typical soldier, and off
the barrack quare he was again like so many of his two-legged
pals: he once nipped and kicked a squadron of artillerymen
and it was always quite a job to keep him in a corral.

Because mules are usually black or brown, he made a great
show on parade, marching smartly and giving the impression
that he knew all eyes were on him. Of the 1,800 mules on the
establishment at Fort Carson, only Hambone and his younger
team-mate ever received any sort of recognition.

It was the difficulty of keeping him in a corral that brought
to light his exceptional jumping ability and the army was not
slow to make capital out of his skill. It is said that he could

stand flat-footed and jump a 5ft fence without touching it. When, like most army types, he got fed up with it all, he would just jump the enclosure fence, but as this occurred with regularity, his handlers could not only predict his disappearances but always knew where to look for him. Usually he was at a nearby farm when the dairy cows were being fed.

Hambone was, in fact, more suited to riding than to pulling heavy artillery, but he had one pet hate and that was the spur. Even the merest touch put him into a mad temper that invariably sent his rider flying. Usually, however, he could get away with his misdemeanours. It is a mystery how he managed during the whole of his army career never to be branded with the traditional US marks on his flank. It was only shortly before he died that his army number '5911' was discovered under the hair of his neck.

He was entered in jumping contests under the name of Hamilton T. Bone, and always had fewer jumping faults notched up against him than the horses he was competing with. So whilst his team mate went on to become a West Point mascot, Hambone found increased fame as a performer at rodeos all over the region. When he first took the field in some of the big horse shows there were raised eyebrows among the committee, and when he won most of the jumping classes they were raised higher still.

His entertaining antics on these occasions won for him an accolade in 1949, when *Life* magazine wrote a special feature on him. In 1954, he was taken to meet Francis, the famous Hollywood mule, but Hambone just snubbed him. There was a little jenny named Mitzi at Fort Carson, whom he taught to jump, but, alas, no romance comes to anything in the life of a mule because they are all sterile.

Hambone's army life came to a close in December 1956, when the last two mule-pack units passed by in a farewell review and the US Army brought to an end its colourful history of artillery mule packs. What the mule's reactions were to leaving the service we shall never know, but as far as the army was concerned parting was sad. Pop Cnossen, Hambone's handler, unashamedly shed tears.

For Hambone a new chapter of life began. He was purchased by the Pikes Peak, a rodeo assocation, and for several years was a star performer in the Range Ride, an annual 100 mile trek through the Rockies. However, the time came when he was no longer able to make the trip, so he went into complete retirement on the Turkey Track ranch owned by Mr J. D. Ackerman. He made just one public appearance from the ranch and that was in 1967, to follow the hearse at the military funeral of his former handler Pop Cnossen.

After fourteen years of civilian life the dear old mule began to show signs of deterioration. He was sent back to Fort Carson, where the vets took good care of him. Nevertheless, he started falling and one morning a heart attack resulted in his death.

Hambone had become a legend, and with old soldiers fellowships are long remembered. Civilians too, particularly children, wished to pay tribute to a friend. A full funeral was inevitable. Post engineers constructed a sturdy wooden box measuring 8 x 3 x 4ft. A 12th Cavalry wrecker vehicle hoisted the box aboard a transporter and at the graveside Hambone was lowered into a 10ft grave which had been dug by the engineers. Later a concrete slab measuring 15 x 18ft was placed over the grave and a rock wall erected, and the formal funeral ceremony took place. Three rounds were fired by a battery of 75mm howitzers, the guns that Hambone had pulled during his army life. The final farewell salute, as for any other soldier of the unit at internment, was taken as the band played 'Mountain Battery'. It will be surprising if there is not a statue erected over the grave in due course.

This great mule gave pleasure to almost all with whom he came into contact during the long years of his life. After all thirty-nine years for a mule is equivalent to 120 years for a two-legged human animal, and few of these are as beloved as Hambone when they die.

ELEPHANTS JOIN THE NAVY

When the British Navy does anything, it does it well, and this is true of its traditional send-offs to retiring captains. One of the best of these was the farewell given to Captain Peter Loasby, skipper of the 6,000-ton guided missile destroyer *London*, when he retired. Portsmouth was all agog when it learned that something special was afoot. This was to be a flotilla in the grand style—and it was, for thirteen elephants joined the navy for the day and turned out to give the captain a jumbo-sized farewell.

The animals were borrowed from Billy Smart's circus, and spick and span they paraded at the jetty. Captain Loasby made a mock inspection of his new ratings and then—not without some difficulty—mounted the leader. Other officers mounted and fell in behind. The captain, dismounting, then took his place in a vintage car and led the procession out of the dock-yard, toasting the crew of his last command as he went.

'He was a popular captain and we wanted to give him a final day he would never forget', said one of his officers. There is no doubt at all that they succeeded. And the elephants, the most regal and dignified of all animals, upheld their tradition too. They behaved perfectly.

Captain Loasby on leaving HMS *London* became ADC to the Queen.

CHARLIE FURY—ROGUE

Bird lovers are often laughed at when they attribute to their pets a thinking power akin to human commonsense. Nevertheless, they are not to be shaken in their belief that birds as well as other pets (even those brought in young from the wild) often seem to divine by some sixth sense the next move of their masters. The strange story of Charlie the crow is a case in point.

Charlie belonged to the Fury family of Abergavenny in Monmouthshire. In their time they have had many pets, which have been discovered in a distressed state and which they have brought back to health. Charlie was found, when he was only a fledgling, by Geoffrey Fury aged fourteen. The bird was in a poor state and had a back claw torn off its leg. The Fury family patched him up, put a perch in an outhouse and fed him regularly with hard-boiled egg. Water was given in a small teaspoon, and Mr Fury, who is disabled and at home all day, was able to attend to this duty at regular intervals. Very soon every time someone stepped out of the back door Charlie would start to caw, and he progressed to hand feeding without difficulty. Then flying lessons began by swinging him off the wrist, and before long he could fly well. At night he was put into an aviary. After a short while he knew bed-time as well as anyone, and he would fly to the aviary on his own. Then he got crafty and at dusk he would avoid the humans and fly to an upstairs window ledge to perch, waking everyone up at daybreak by tapping at the window. Then he would wait till the room was empty, fly in through the top ventilating windows and begin to create havoc.

Life was a glorious game in which he seemed to know every move and be able to anticipate it. If, for instance, the Furys were going out and went up to the bedroom to change, Charlie would be off and away to the end of the road to await them there. When they arrived, he would follow them, and often he accompanied Mrs Fury shopping.

Charlie soon had a repertoire of amusing and terrible tricks. A game he enjoyed, and would play for hours, was tug-of-war with a piece of string. Less enjoyable to the other parties was his game of flying down and pecking at the back legs of the dogs. One day he did this once too often, for he pecked a terrier bitch with small puppies. The terrier turned, pinned him down and all but killed him. The miscreant had to be brought round with brandy. Fighting fit again, he avoided the terrier but gave the cats a miserable life. Twisting the end of their tails in his beak was a favourite pastime. He was also a skilled dive bomber, swooping down from above and drawing his claws over their heads.

This black bundle of mischief had a habit of collecting things and, while everyone was very fond of the bird and apt to laugh at his antics, he went too far—much too far—when he made off with a set of dentures left in a glass, and carried them up to the roof. Eventually they were recovered. Clothes lines and pegs had a particular attraction for him and he could get most pegs off the line, often with disastrous consequences. Any object that caught his eye was picked up. Some he would bury, others he would use to line the gulley between the path and the lawn. Then he would hover above, look down and enjoy to the full his collection of buttons, silver paper, milk bottle tops and other odds and ends.

His escapades were endless, and his obvious sense of fun soon brought the family round to laughing at him, no matter how angry they were at first. One day three pork chops were left in a momentarily deserted kitchen. Charlie had them on the roof in no time at all. Next day one neighbour lost a bacon rasher and another found that six ounces of cheese (Charlie's favourite delicacy) had mysteriously disappeared.

Charlie had one fear, however: he was scared of other crows. If he saw one he would head for home at speed, cawing loudly and continuously. The other crows behaved as they usually do with a drop-out from their own society, and were angry and vicious.

The Fury family got a lot of fun from Charlie, but some of the neighbours only had the rough side of things. One old man living opposite was pestered by repeated knockings on his door, and when he opened it no one was there. At last, however, the culprit was caught—it was Charlie. He was seen hooking his claws in the knocker, flapping his wings and then

letting the knocker drop. Then off he went to a hidden point
of vantage to watch the door open. And then he would start
all over again. Charlie, rather disappointed at being discovered, then added insult to injury by dive-bombing the old
chap's head. This became an obsession with Charlie and not
all the neighbours shared his sense of humour, particularly
when he perched on their hats. He loved millinery, particularly when it was in transit.

Complaints gathered ground and the neighbours appealed
to the local council. Consequently the Furys were admonished
and warned to keep the bird under control.

The end of the story is a sad one. As is obvious, Charlie
was never caged or confined in any way; he flew round freely
but always returned for his food and to roost at night. One
day, not long after his story had appeared in the newspapers,
he flew home injured and shortly afterwards died. The veterinary surgeon who was called in found an air-gun pellet in
him. A lad living nearby said he had heard three shots from
an air-gun and the crow, which was perched on a post,
screeched and flew off. The Furys took the case to court and
the owner of the air-gun, a journalist aged eighteen, was
charged with wilfully injuring a wild bird. The case was dis-
missed on inconclusive evidence. The Fury family and quite
a lot of the neighbours miss Charlie, for he was a great character and the world is dolefully lacking in characters, great
or small.

AN AFFINITY WITH CAXTON

We are continually hearing of the queer things that birds do.
There was the hen, for instance, who fluttered up to the spare
wheel under the tail board of a lorry while the driver was at
lunch; when he returned he drove right off to Bristol, quite
oblivious of the fact that he had a travelling companion tak-

ing her first trip. When the bird was discovered, the driver took her up into the cab with him for the return journey, considering it less precarious. The hen showed her gratitude by laying an egg on the seat beside him. The big wide world obviously fascinated the hen, for a week or so later she did the same journey and paid the same price. Her fame will never dim now, for a pub near Bristol has been named after her—the Travelling Hen.

Birds nest in the most unexpected places, but quite inexplicable was the choice of a pair of robins who built their nest and reared six youngsters right by the machines in a busy printing works. It happened in a Devonshire town during the Easter holidays, when the robins found that by entering between the louvres high up in the wall, they had the factory to themselves. If they resented the intrusion when the men returned to work, they did not show it. The partly built nest was discovered in what was thought to be a precarious position, so the foreman carefully removed it and fixed it on the top of a 6ft plank, which he stood on end so that it was out of harm's way.

The robins, however, must have had an irresistible affinity with William Caxton for they promptly abandoned the partly built nest and immediately began another at a spot equidistant between three fast running machines and only 4ft above the floor. What is more, they abandoned their first way in and chose an easier one through the open windows. Nest building went on apace in the corner of a cardboard box and the men put a tray over the top of it for safety. With unabated zeal the birds flew in and out all day and every day. Before going direct to the nest, they would alight on one or other of the machines and take stock. Printers' ink worried them not at all, for sometimes they would pause on the inked rollers and every operative had to check carefully before he started up in case the movement should engulf the birds.

Eventually the nest was finished and the hen occupied it. Every morning there was keen competition by the printers to

see who could bring the best tit-bits to put on saucers outside
the nest. It began to look like a harvest festival. Wars and
rumours of wars, strikes and lockouts—all would have taken
second place to the well being of the nesting birds. The first
enquiry every morning was: 'What's happened—everything
all right?'

Then came the morning when the first egg appeared; five
more soon followed. The incubation period was a time of
great trial to everyone in the building, particularly at one
short period when the hen left the nest for some hours. But
eventually the eggs were hatched and soon the youngsters
made their appearance on trial flights. Sad to say, all did not
go well and for some days two or three of the fledglings were
missing, to be found later in the boiler room: first one, then
others were found dead on the floor. The one fortunate survivor flew off.

So did the parents, but for a day or two only. They returned
and started to build a new nest, this time high up in the angle
of the metal work of the north-light roof. The printers were
worried men. 'What', they asked, 'will happen when trial
flights begin for any new youngsters?' There was a sheer 40ft
drop below the nest and no branches to break the fall. They
need not have worried, for the birds apparently thought that
one out too. Abruptly they stopped building and started work
on a new nest again in a cardboard box, but a little higher
than the first nest. It was duly completed; eggs were laid and
hatched; and all the processes were again watched over by the
humans.

Eventually the fledglings were given flying lessons by the
parents, up and down the length of the printing works. One
by one in succeeding days they made their exits through the
top windows.

The story, however, does not end there. The adult robins
still come in for titbits, but fly out with them—so the youngsters cannot be far away.

SQUAWKER IS THE BOSS

Following the plough too closely caused the downfall of Squawker the black-headed seagull. At least this seems the only possible explanation for a gull found lying in the middle of a country road with its wing sheared off. Mrs D. Northwood of Rushden in Northamptonshire came upon it one evening and carried the bird home in the rather forlorn hope that they would be able to do something for it. For a while they had to resort to force feeding, and then after much trial and error, discovered that maggots from a fishing-tackle shop went down well.

The bird began to perk up and take stock of his surroundings. There were friends and playmates to hand, two children, two dogs—Sherry and Buster—and six cats—Ming, Yasmin, Tabby, Fluffy, Paws and Dusty—quite an assortment for any gull, especially one that could not fly. Very soon he reserved for himself an old knitted skirt, and regarding it as his territory was prepared to defend it against all comers, including the children and cats. They soon found that it was indiscreet to go too close. This behaviour led Mrs Northwood to think that perhaps Squawker was after all a 'she' and was in effect defending her nest.

Sherry, the nine-year-old labrador, and one of her offspring, Buster, had long ago become used to accepting strays for, after all, four of the cats had been adopted one by one in the same manner. The only two real residents were the Siamese, Ming and Yasmin.

So Squawker took up residence and settled in, commuting freely between house and garden all day and staying in the house by choice at night. The rug in front of the hearth is a favourite spot, as is the garden for a nap among the flowers with the cats, though a shower of rain is enough to send the gull indoors. If there is a possibility of food Squawker is always on the spot, and when Mrs Northwood returns from

shopping the bird invariably takes up her station by the door
of the fridge.

Squawker's desire to get up on to the sofa seemed doomed
to failure, for with only one wing the jump was beyond her.
But she discovered that by hopping on to Sherry's back the
next jump was easily made. Jumping off the garden wall without over-balancing was, to start with, no mean feat. She
worked out her own routine to get up to the garden wall, a
favourite vantage point. It was too high for one jump so she
made a detour to the bottom of the garden where it was lower,
and then walked along the top.

Gradually Squawker has become the boss. If the cats are
away over long, they are told off in no uncertain manner when
they return. With lowered head she runs at them squawking.

The Northwood household has other visitors which are befriended strays. One of these is a baby crow which used to
divide his time between chasing the cats round the garden and
flying into the house. Then he vanished for a period of eight
days and reappeared on the ninth waking the household with
loud caws at 5.40 am. He spent the morning about the house
but flew off later. It is a timetable he often repeats.

A tawny baby owl with two broken legs was picked up by
a member of the family. He is the real 'glamour' boy of the
household and happily has responded to treatment—though
whether he will be fit enough to go back to the wild state is
open to question.

Over them all Squawker maintains a benevolent rule.

FATE AND FAVOUR

CAT FALLS FROM STEEPLE

Mr A. E. Watts is the Chief Inspector of the mid-Sussex and Brighton branch of the Royal Society for the Prevention of Cruelty to Animals, and like the rest of his colleagues he never knows as each day dawns what queer twists, surprises and even dangers his job will bring.

On one occasion a cat was reported in the steeple of a disused church at Dyke Road, Brighton. Mr Watts climbed up from the inside but was unable to locate the animal. Day followed day and the cat could be heard crying but could not be seen. On the ninth day it seemed that the cat's cry was now coming from the outside of the steeple, and that night a lady living nearby caught sight of the cat's eyes in the dark. She telephoned Mr Watts, who managed to pinpoint the animal with the aid of a powerful torch. Nothing could be done until next morning when another climb up the inside of the steeple revealed a small hole through which the cat had scrambled to the outside, where it was somehow managing to retain a precarious foothold right at the top of the steeple, 120ft from the ground.

The fire brigade was then contacted but the turntable ladder proved to be too short by a few feet, so a 16ft metal grasper was obtained. The idea was to get this round the cat's neck and draw it to the top table of the ladder. All went well, while the crowd of onlookers below held their breath; but just as success was in sight, the cat, in dodging the grasper, lost its hold. The very length of the implement made it unmanageable at the top of a ladder, and Inspector Watts on the ground below saw that the cat was going to fall. The animal came hurtling down at a terrific speed, and quickly gauging the distance, the inspector made a dive for its probable landing place and by a miracle caught the cat in his arms. The impact almost broke his wrists.

Immediately dubbed Lucky, the cat was taken to the RSPCA clinic and given treatment. It was found that no bones were broken, though it was terribly thin after its eight days in the steeple, and it had probably been a stray before that. Unfortunately Lucky became ill, developed pneumonia, and in spite of its new name and all the care and attention it received it died four days after being rescued.

SURELY MINETTE'S NINTH LIFE!

When a six-month-old cat has already expended several of her lives on an 8,560 mile voyage by raft, she can reasonably expect to be received on dry land with a degree of acclamation. But black-and-white Minette was to all intents and purposes clapped into irons and given a death sentence when she landed in Australia a year or so ago.

Her raft, *La Balsa*, with its four-man crew made land near Brisbane after a voyage of five months' duration. Health officials seized Minette, put her in a cage, placed her in quarantine, and passed sentence of death within twenty-four hours because she came from Ecuador where rabies was prevalent.

Captain Vital Alsar, Spanish-Mexican skipper of the raft, said that they had set out with four cats and four parrots and Minette was the only survivor. Indeed, she had been washed overboard many times, but members of the crew dived into the sea and rescued her. The Australian authorities were however, adamant in their resolve that Minette must die, and the pleadings of the crew seemed of no avail. The *Sunday Express* in Brisbane reported that hope had almost been given up when Captain Charles Helleman of the 8,000-ton Swedish cargo ship, *Cirrus*, joined the fray and declared that he would willingly have the cat on his ship rather than see her destroyed as a prohibited immigrant.

The port officials relented and permitted the cat to board the *Cirrus*, with instructions that she was not to be allowed out of her cage until the ship was outside territorial waters. Captain Helleman agreed and promised that they would either give Minette a home until the crew of the raft wanted her back, when they would drop her off at the nearest port or they would keep her with them on the high seas for the rest of her life. And as this is surely her last life it is to be hoped that the cargo ship proves more comfortable and less hazardous than *La Balsa·*

Minette deserves her good fortune, for under Captain Alsar she had helped to prove that it was possible for ancient man to have voyaged from South America to the other side of the world by raft. The other members of the crew were Marc Modena, a Frenchman, at forty-three the oldest member of the expedition, Gabriel Salas of Chile, and Norman Tetreault, a Canadian.

TOBY AND THE TAX MAN

The human race has come to accept taxes as part of the way of life. In the New Testament we read: 'And it came to pass in those days that there went out a decree from Caesar Augustus, that all the world should be taxed'. George Smollet in 1770, alluded to the levying of taxes: 'The inevitable conse

Page 53 *(above)* Josephine the lioness in thoughtful mood at Windsor Safari Park (page 97); *(below)* Pharoah the lion takes Lord Gretton for a walk (page 101)

Page 54 *(above)* The amazing friendship of the Rhode Island Red and the stray cat (page 11); *(below)* Tiger Tim in inquisitive mood

quences of being too fond of glory: Taxes upon every article
which enters into the mouth or covers the back, or placed
under the foot...taxes upon everything on earth and the
waters under the earth'. And in 1789 Benjamin Franklin
wrote: 'But in this world nothing can be said to be certain
except death and taxes'.

So if he could read and understand the queer ways of
humans, Toby, a cheerful, fourteen-year-old mongrel, would
appreciate that he, too, is covered by these utterances. For
Toby the dog pays income tax at the standard rate.

Toby was due to be destroyed as a stray when Mrs Weale
took him in, because as she said, he was so lovable and she
could not resist him. With her he lived a life of luxury and
only the best was good enough for master Toby, but he never
became pampered and was a lively, cheerful little chap who
had a host of friends. Among these friends were the small sons
of her neighbour, Mrs D. Hulbert, and whenever he heard
the lads playing ball he whined and scratched until he could
be let out to join in their game.

The years went by and when illness overtook his mistress
she asked Mrs Hulbert to look after Toby for as long as he
lived, and made a will leaving £1 ($2.60) a week for his keep.
Naturally Mrs Hulbert and her sons had become extremely
fond of Toby over the years, but they insisted in vain that
they would be happy to accept responsibility for him without
any sort of payment.

Eventually the dog's mistress died and Toby moved in with
the neighbour. After the first year's annuity had been paid
HM Inspector of Taxes wrote:

> It is regretted that no relief is due in respect of the annuity left
> for the care and maintenance of your deceased friend's dog.
> Liability to tax is due at the standard rate on any annuity less
> any allowance given to a person. Of course, the dog does not
> qualify as a person.

Mrs Hulbert was rather incensed. For one thing, she spends
90p a week on Toby's food, but, more important than that she

D

thought it disgraceful that the tax-man should grab money left by an old lady for her sole companion for years—her dog. Nevertheless, the Chancellor of the Exchequer makes off with £22.25 of the £52 ($135) a year left for Toby's maintenance. Mrs Hulbert complained to the local tax office and—need we say?—to no avail.

Toby is fortunately oblivious of the injustice done to him; otherwise he might add the tax collector to his pet dislikes—cats and motor-cyclists (and if he did, he would have a lot of sympathisers). Meanwhile, he enjoys life, particularly when there is a ball game going on.

Recently when workmen were digging a hole in the road, he took a lively interest and when the hole got really deep he fetched his ball and dropped it in. Naturally the men did what they were expected to do and threw it out. Toby scampered off, collected it and dropped it into the hole again. After several repetitions of this, the foreman complained that much as Toby was enjoying himself he was holding up the work, and requested that the dog be kept in the house while the job was in progress. Toby had to wait until Mrs Hulbert could take him down to the river where, being a fine swimmer, he retrieves sticks that are thrown until his companion —never Toby—tires.

So Toby pays his tax by proxy and enjoys life, and Mrs Hulbert, except on the point of principle, would not have it any other way.

CANDY HAS A SWEET TOOTH

Candy the Welsh corgi was born in 1959. Reddish in colour, his white socks were a distinction which just had to be added to his high-sounding pedigree name to make him Larkwhistle Lucifer Whitesox. When he was just on a year old he had to be found a new home, and so came to Bedford.

On that first night in his new home he was in trouble, for he jumped on his mistress's bed and refused to budge until finally dislodged with a tennis racquet, but after that he needed little correction. He soon learned to go and fetch anything that was wanted in the house and showed a considerable degree of intelligence.

He was an upright character for many years—until his mistress was about to be married. Candy watched with interest the many and varied preparations being made for the event, and when it came to the making of the wedding-cake, he was absolutely intrigued. He sat by his mistress's side as the ingredients were mixed and, like so many other pets, looked on longingly until he was given some. Obviously what he tasted he liked. His interest remained unabated up to the stage when the marzipan was carefully added to the third and last tier, and all was ready for the icing.

Then his mistress, Jean Jones, wrapped the cake in foil, covered it again with a cloth, placed it on a table and went out for just half an hour, leaving Candy and two cats in the house. Opening the front door on her return, Miss Jones was met by a trail of tin foil which led her, alas, to the remains—and only the remains—of her beautiful cake. Candy was called to no avail, but eventually they found him hiding in a corner of another room with bits of the marzipan between his sticky paws. He had evidently reached saturation point for by now the cats, too, were partaking of the pre-wedding feast. Somewhat naturally, the bride-to-be was furious, so cross indeed that Candy received a smack on the nose. There was nothing for it but set to and make another cake.

Now all is forgiven. Miss Jones is Mrs O'Dell, and Candy has moved in with the newly-weds.

THE AMERICAN CASTAWAY

It was mid-winter when the New York City harbour patrol

reported that they had seen a dog on Ruffle Bar, a tiny un-inhabited island in the bay, between Brooklyn and Queens. It was a bleak and swampy piece of land, without trees, vegetation or shelter.

When as a result of the report, enquiries were made, one patrolman said he had seen a dog on the island on and off for two years. The American Society for the Prevention of Cruelty to Animals heard the story and fearing for the animal's health visited the place in a police launch. The weather prevented the boat from getting within 100ft of the shoal surrounding the island, so they completed the journey by rowing boat, scouted the desolate island and saw the dog on the far side but could not get to it because of the waist-deep swamp.

Two days later, this time fully equipped for the job, they tried again, and finally left a humane trap baited with food on a hillock. The police helicopter branch was asked to make a daily check but it was nine days before the dog was seen actually in the cage. The news received, a boat set off immediately and brought the animal ashore to the ASPCA hospital. The patient, who proved to be a female German sheepdog, had no injuries other than a broken tooth and worn toenails, but appeared to be almost starving. Nevertheless, she weighed 50lb and the vets agreed that her relatively good condition indicated that she could not have been marooned for any great length of time—probably a few weeks or, at most, a few months.

She was soon christened Ruffles (from the name of the island) and after careful attention for a week or so was ready to receive callers. Naturally such a story hit the newspaper and television headlines, and a whole host of people seemed to think that the dog was their long-lost pet, so a steady stream of visitors arrived to see her. Most of the time Ruffles sat motionless, not barking and seemingly completely oblivious to the noise or movement of other animals round her.

None of the visitors recognised the dog however, and she remained unclaimed. The Society began to sift through the many offers of adoption that had been received. Eventually Mr and Mrs J. De George were chosen as the ideal adopters. They had two boys, aged thirteen and ten, another German sheepdog, Misty, six cats and two horses, and $2\frac{1}{2}$ acres for them to roam in. Ruffles soon settled down and became one of the family, and within a short while the two dogs were inseparable.

One of Ruffles' favourite pastimes is digging tunnels, not just holes in the ground but real ones, sometimes 5ft or 6ft long. The family cover them up as soon as they are discovered, as they fear she may get trapped in one, but they are convinced that it was this love of digging that saved the dog's life on the island for she probably holed up in one during the fearful weather. When they go for a swim, Ruffles only goes in to a depth of about 12in, then sits and surveys the scene. Perhaps she is thinking she has seen enough water, and who could blame her?

Ruffles the dog, with Ruffle the island now firmly behind her, is—to quote the family—'one of us', and it should be added, a handsome one at that. It was a lucky sighting by the patrolman, and another instance of the splendid work carried on by the ASPCA.

It is also another fascinating imponderable. How did Ruffles get to the island? Did she swim? Did she walk over the ice? Was she perhaps left by picnickers the previous summer? Having got to the island, how did she exist? It is doubtful if she could have survived by catching the odd seagull. Finally, what went on in the dog's mind? Her behaviour when rescued was very much that of a human in similar circumstances—a kind of dazed indifference to her surroundings.

A CASTLE REFUGE

In the Middle Ages a nobleman's castle would serve as a

haven to the people of nearby villages in time of trouble. The retainers, of course, resided there all the time. Something like this happens to this day at Dacre Castle in Cumberland, except that now it is animals and birds who look for peace beneath its strong walls.

When Bunty and Anthony Kinsman left London to take possession of the deserted and neglected twelfth-century castle, they little thought that in next to no time they would be affording refuge to so many 'neighbours', in addition to their own pets. They had reckoned without their ten-year-old daughter Sapphia, who finds it impossible to refuse succour to any maimed or helpless creature who comes or is brought to her. But indeed all Sapphia's family—her parents, her elder sister Amanda, and her two younger brothers Ivan and Sebastian—love birds and animals.

Here at Dacre Castle colonies of budgerigars and canaries fly entirely free. They have an aviary in the castle's outbuildings with a funnel which is permanently open. The canaries, which have been crossed with siskins, are of a startingly attractive light golden colour. They all, particularly the canaries, demand attention, and when they tire of tapping on the windows of the castle requesting entrance, they fly down and perch on the outsize door knocker, as though knowing that eventually someone must come in or out, thereby giving them the chance of a crafty entrance. There were once even more of the canaries and the budgerigars, but unfortunately some forty of them fled in terror when Guy Fawkes night was celebrated nearby and they have never been seen since.

It is Sapphia who has steeped herself in budgerigar lore and has read and re-read a mighty tome, the *Cult of the Budgerigar*. When she returns from school at weekends the family do not know which they fear most, her indignation at something amiss with the birds or her astonishment at their complete inability to identify one from the other among the large family. She is now at work on a most complicated family tree of the birds.

Sometimes a sparrow finds its way into the aviary and fails to remember the way out. It takes but a short time then for it to be joined by a dozen or so of its fellows, and they all seem unable to find the exit, whereas the canaries and budgerigars are never at a loss.

The Castle peacocks and peahens, magnificent specimens, are real characters. The vanity of the three cocks has to be seen to be believed, and they particularly like to perch and strut where they can see their reflections. So when a nice shiny limousine drives up to the castle, it is not uncommon for them to jump on it and bask in their own reflected glory, to the great embarrassment of the family, who often have a lot of explaining to do. At first the peacocks used to fly off to visit chicken farms in the area, presumably to be admired by mere common-or-garden hens, but it was found that a looking-glass put at a vantage point in the barn stopped these excursions. At night, in the barn, the cocks perch on the foremost roof truss, while the thirteen peahens dutifully take the truss behind; as Bunty comments wryly, there is no room for Women's Lib in the peacock's world.

When the peahen's chicks are hatched, no time at all is lost in teaching them to fly. There seems almost a panic crash programme to get them off the ground, due no doubt to fear of marauding foxes. Four weeks would seem the limit for lessons, and should there be backward pupils after that, the hens have been seen to encourage the chicks to fly on to their backs and then they soar up to the roof with them.

At Dacre Castle far more faith is placed in the peacocks as weather forecasters than in the pundits at the meteorological office. If the weather is going to be fair, the peacocks will roost in a tall ash tree, but their retirement to the barn warns all who care to heed that bad weather is in the offing. Their antics to get to the taller branches of the tree are amusing to watch, for they take the first lap up to the barn roof with ease; the next move obviously requires some forethought as to whether they can manoeuvre their tails through the branches on the next sally and they spend much time in noisy debate of the point.

The fascinating story of the move from London and the gradual building-up of this modern Noah's ark, is told in Bunty Kinsman's own book *Pawn takes Castle.* Here we read about the exotic ducks acquired to keep the moorhens company; about albino hares and the handsome Saluki who, alas, failed one day to overcome his hunting instincts and claimed a sheep. The story of their donkey, docile when purchased but who at the sight of the battlements turned into a bucking bronco and threw the children from his back, is delightfully told, as is the case of the unwanted peachick that became delinquent. A sad note creeps in when Mrs Kinsman comments on the devasting results of insecticides on the wild bird population.

There are four dogs on the castle establishment. Two are whippets and one a crossbred sheepdog, Moss, who has taken upon himself the duty of guarding the children. No retainer of old in the castle's long history ever took his duties more seriously. He walks miles with them over the fells and while they are at home is a watchman par excellence. He adores the girls but is less keen on the males. When the time comes for them all to leave for school, one would think Moss could relax, secure in the knowledge that his duty has been done. Not a bit of it, he just lies about and sulks until the youngsters return.

The fourth dog is an eleven-year-old Yorkshire terrier, Andrew, who was taken in when a friend became incapacitated. Andrew was becoming something of a cross between an inebriated old gentleman and a hypochondriac, because he had learned that the right look in his eyes, and merest movement of his tail and a cough always brought his master hurrying with relief in the form of a spoonful of brandy and glycerine. He liked it so much that he coughed nearly all day. At first the Kinsmans found it difficult to win him away from his favourite tipple. However, when he found that he coughed

Page 63 *(above)* The fox and Quintin the hedgehog share a nocturnal meal
(page 12); *(below)* Hambone, the lovable mule (page 38)

Page 64 *(above)* Sapphia Kinsman and the bird of prey she rescued. Note the torn wing (page 63); *(below)* Donald MacCastill with his polecat which he is successfully rearing

age 65   Sally, aged twenty-six, the skewbald mare that was rescued (page 87)

Page 66   *(above)* Canine Ben-Hurs; *(below)* the age of innocence

nd looked soulful in vain, he eventually became resigned to
is fate. Now he is quite a reformed character.

Bantam gamecocks and their families are legion in the
astle courtyard· They are handsome fellows but their num-
ers increase by leaps and bounds for the hens lay their eggs
n unusual places and never in the same place twice, with the
esult that at regular intervals a new brood that no one knew
nything about is led proudly in. The chicks are absolute
uplicates of their miniature mothers, and they really do look
picture.

The Kinsman family go for long walks over the fells and up
o Martindale forest, often camping out, and it is on these
ccasions that there are often surprise meetings. The occa-
ional deer, a fox, even a badger are fairly commonplace, but
t is most unusual to discover, as they did, a tortoise measur-
ng some 12in from stem to stern twenty miles from any-
here. This tortoise was brought back and was content
nough for a while, then he (or she) wandered off to the woods
nd is now seen only occasionally.

Pets are legion in this delightful corner of Cumberland.
ome have a short stay, some settle down. There was Edward
he pet lamb, who lost his mother and was fed by bottle five
imes a day. Another was the sparrowhawk with the damaged
ing who was responding to treatment and really seemed to
ppreciate what was being done for him. Unfortunately, to-
ards the end of his convalescence, when he gave way to his
atural instinct and dived on a bird he did it from too low an
ltitude and broke his neck.

Among the horses at Dacre Castle is the children's pony
ixie. Like so many of his kind he has a love and understand-
ng of children. On very special occasions he has been known
o mount the stairs and gatecrash a party.

For the Kinsman family life is full of surprises. What better
lace for them than this lovely countryside where herons and
agles nest and where the mood of nearby Ullswater is never
he same for two minutes together. It seems to matter little

whether Andrew has his brandy or the sparrows do effect a
break-in, or the tortoise waddles away.

FROM KENNEL TO CASTLE

When Kathy was a tiny puppy her large head and feet would
have suggested to someone well used to dogs that she was
likely to grow into a large animal. But the lorry driver who
first purchased her as a companion was not that discerning
and as she grew and grew he was too fond of her to let her go
until he lost his job—and then there was no alternative. He
took her therefore to Mr Glascoe, who runs an animal sanctuary at Borough Green in Kent and left her, with the warning
that no kennel or fence would hold her. Kathy was now fully
grown, and a fully grown Pyrenean mountain dog at that!

Mr Glascoe had a job on his hands! People were prepared
to take a chance over such a magnificent animal, but although
eight different homes were found for her she stayed at none
of them. The last owner was a Kent farmer and he returned
Kathy to Mr Glascoe after she had smashed the windows of
the house to get out and then made her way to the M20 motorway, where she was nothing short of a menace.

Kathy in her short lifetime had already become famous.
She had appeared on the Blue Peter children's television programme, to highlight for children the problems of owning a
large dog, special emphasis being placed on the size of her
food bill. Her story, with pictures, had also made headlines
in the press. This publicity saved the situation, for just as Mr
Glascoe was feeling desperate and utterly despondent, he
received out of the blue an instruction which read:

> On no account have Kathy put to sleep. Put her on a flight from
> Heathrow addressed to: The Duchess of Alba, The Palace,
> Madrid.

He confesses to feeling an immense relief, for it really had looked as if the end of the road was looming for Kathy. Her food bill alone was a problem: weighing 115lb, with a 36in girth and standing 29in high, she made short work of a basic daily allowance of one pint of milk, 2lb cooked meat and 12oz biscuit.

The Duchess of Alba, who confesses to a weakness for stray dogs, had read about Kathy in a newspaper and immediately made arrangements for her to be sent to Madrid. Kathy's new home is a 100-room castle, occupying a site of 25 acres. She was settled down happily with the family and the other dogs in the establishment.

It is a traditionally happy ending to the story of Kathy the princess (albeit canine) and the fairy-tale castle.

HONEY THE HORNBLOWER

A disturbing number of people have pets and, beyond seeing them about the house, take no further notice of them. Typical was the case of a black and tan mongrel named Trixie. She belonged to some flat dwellers who were out at work all day and left the unfortunate animal to her own devices. Eventually they decided to get rid of her and advertised for a new home.

The subsequent story comes from Eileen Edgar, of Annan in Dumfriesshire, Scotland, whose family decided they would get a companion for granny. They collected Trixie and drove home by car. The dog's amazement at the sight of the big, wide world will ever remain in their memory. She must have been out before, but by her reactions it must have been quite a rarity and at eighteen months she was not even house-trained. She was afraid of almost everything, but was soon absorbed into the family and settled down happily, eagerly exploring all the new exciting objects around her.

A ball was obviously a completely new toy, and chocolate was manna from heaven. Equally strange to her were other dogs, but these she soon accepted except, for some obscure reason, white ones. Naturally cats had been provided by Providence to be run after, and one she chased the length of the garden until the quarry found safety by shinning up a tree. Honey sat at the foot for a while, then like a man taking a high jump ran back the length of the garden and made a terrific dash, hoping to gain enough impetus to get up the trunk. Her failure to accomplish this obviously not only puzzled her but injured her pride. But she was a trier. At intervals she again and again made the effort and finally one day hit on the bright idea of jumping up on the wall, running along and then taking a flying leap into the tree. Her rapid descent through the branches to the ground certainly disconcerted her; but Honey, being Honey, has not given up this adventure yet.

One day while waiting in the car when the family were shopping, she accidentally put her paw on the horn and quickly realised that this brought someone running. Now she has it all organised. She will allow them reasonable latitude but anything over fifteen minutes and she puts a paw on the horn button and keeps it there until someone returns to keep her company.

Perhaps her most endearing trait is her concern for every one when the family are off for a drive. Always first in, she then looks round and counts heads. If anyone is delayed or missing, out she jumps again and will not get back until they are all there.

Though when she first went to her new home she was terrified even of a sweeping brush, she now looks forward to having the Hoover brush run over her coat. Living near the Solway Firth, she often gets down to the water, which she adores, and her swimming ability make the family wonder whether she should not really have webbed feet.

Honey is lucky in her new home, but what pleasure her

previous owners missed in the company of such an attractive animal.

THE CHIFFONIER'S DOG

Most owners get fun and amusement from their pets, but few can derive more enjoyment from them than Mrs Margaret Colling, who now lives at Biot in France. All her life Mrs Colling has had a number of dogs, cats and birds and she has been greatly interested in studying their characters and the amusing differences there are between them.

In France her 'family' commenced with a mongrel she found in the dogs' home at Cannes on the French Riviera. He was in a large run with about forty others, all howling and barking. But this one refused to join in the hullaballoo and remained aloof, pressed up against the wire netting, pleading with his eyes to be let out—large amber eyes, with a coat of a shiny yellow colour and a curly tail to match! When he got to his new home he was amazed at his luck and his gratitude always seemed apparent. His previous life must have been very hard for he had belonged to a drunken 'chiffonier', or rag-and-bone man, which was, of course, why his new owner called him Chiffon. In his new surroundings he soon proved to be loyal, proud, brave and very independent. But he was a clever escapee, for if he detected a bitch in the vicinity neither an 8ft wire fence nor a 20ft drop would deter or defeat him. The house doors with their varying types of handles very soon presented no problem to him at all and he opened them at will.

Bijou, a poodle, came next. She was discovered in a London store. Again the inevitable happened, for she too was the odd one out, and instead of joining in a romp with her brothers and sisters stood on her hind legs, looking at the outside world. She was to prove a show-off for the rest of her life and made the most of every opportunity for performing her 'begging' act, particularly in shops and restaurants. No one ever taught her the trick and none of her numerous descendants ever acquired it. She accompanied the family on their travels across the Continent, lived in Paris, Switzerland, Italy and on small boats for two years, and then had her first litter out of which Mink was retained.

Mink was a complete contrast to her mother. She loved hunting and country life, and loathed cities. One of her particular tricks was to carry a bone or titbit in a certain direction, and then, when spotted, abruptly change direction to find a more secret spot. Two more Colling family poodles were aptly christened Napoleon and Nelson. They spent a lifetime squabbling.

The different characteristics and foibles of the dogs are fascinating to watch. Of six dogs the males, strange to say, are frightened of thunder, gun shy and abhor heights or water, whilst the females do not turn a hair. Quite remarkable, however, is the way they recognise places they have not been to for years, miles away from their home. Immediately they arrive they fall into routines they had adopted when last there, the intervening months or years not seeming to affect the memory in any way.

Mrs Colling relates a touching incident concerning a stray cat that she picked up and took home with her. Obviously too small to look after herself, she was put in a run with a white rabbit. The two soon became great pals and used to roll over and play together; they shared food and even sleeping quarters. The time came when the rabbit died, and the cat just could not understand this. She went over and shook the rabbit again and again, obviously completely overcome by the mystery of her playmate's unresponsiveness.

Mrs Colling derives tremendous fun and pleasure from her animal family. Naturally she suffers much heartache and sorrow when eventually an animal she has befriended or rescued

dies; like most pet-owners she feels that on balance it is she
who is in the animals' debt and not vice versa.

SAMSON GREETS THE VIPs

When the Archbishop of Canterbury, Dr Michael Ramsey,
had celebrated his tenth anniversary as Primate with a service
at the cathedral, one of the first to greet him on his return to
the Old Palace was Samson the labrador. Royalty, church
dignitaries and other distinguished visitors have all been
greeted by Samson in the six years he has been resident at the
Old Palace. He was born of champion parents and is a
tremendous character, very intelligent, and a constant and
devoted companion.

He grew up side by side with Silsoe, a Siamese cat, and
they became boon companions. Once when the cat was missing for three days Samson was desolate and mooned about the
palace showing his obvious distress. But Silsoe had inadvert-
ently been shut up in the cathedral crypt, and when the
verger entered carrying the truant, Samson went wild with
delight. He picked him up as he would a rabbit and hurried
to deposit him to the kitchen, where he barked long and
loudly until food was produced for his companion.

Whilst he takes his duties as host very seriously, he enjoys a
game—particularly with children, who can pull him about at
will—and, like all dogs, revels in his daily walk across the
fields. When the gong sounds for meals, Samson, wherever he
is, makes his way into the dining room and, realising he must
be on his dignity, lies down under the table until the meal is
over and it is time for a romp.

The Archbishop and Mrs Ramsey travel to Canterbury
most weekends and when Samson sees the preparations being
made for their arrival he runs to and from the door listening
for the car so that he can be the first to greet them, almost
wagging his tail off in the process.

Samson is very popular, greeting alike all who visit the Old Palace and the roadmen and farm workers he meets on his walks. Strange that despite this abundant friendliness, he should above all excel as a watchdog.

LITTLE TERRIER WITH A BIG HEART

Down in Devon, the true home of the Jack Russell terriers, they still talk of the sheer 'guts' of Midge, a ten-year-old bitch of that breed who came through many adventures, including swimming a strong tidal river which has always defeated expert human swimmers. Midge was her name and she came to her owner, Mr Donald Pyatt of Exmouth, when she was only a few months old. From her early days she was a winner at terrier shows, nearly always surpassing the Welsh, Lakeland and Border breeds.

Midge had a fondness for the chase and often would sit up on the saddle of Bertie Hill, the Olympic rider. At full gallop Midge would not only hold on but get into the motion of the horse.

Mr Pyatt's family spent many holidays aboard barges on the Midland canals, and Midge loved this. She would sit up in the bow for hours on end watching intently for water rats in the banks, and woe betide them if ever she got near them, which she frequently did by jumping overboard!

At home Mr Pyatt and his two sons were sailing enthusiasts and were frequently out on the river Exe. On one occasion they were going up river with Midge as usual perched up in the bow, for all the world like a ship's figurehead. The wind was against the tide and the dinghy may have jibbed, but it all happened so quickly that nobody really knew. One minute the dog was there and the next she had vanished beneath the water. To any one with a knowledge of the estuary under the conditions then prevailing, this signalled the end of Midge.

Page 75 *(above)* Owner collecting mare and a new foal (page 88); *(below)* Strictly in confidence!

Page 76 *(above)* Dolphins at Windsor Safari Park. They are believed to have more brain than any other animal (page 100); *(below)* The English otter has practically been hunted out of existence; otters are now being imported from India (page 101)

So certain was her owner of her inability to survive that the next morning at dawn he was searching the cockle beds (large expanses of mud along the banks of the estuary) for her body. When Midge slipped overboard, however, she was by no means finished. Three hours later, she stumbled ashore at Dawlish Warren, a peninsula at the mouth of the river and at least two miles from her point of entry. She walked up the beach and was spotted by a lad, a member of the local sailing club, who knew her. She was soaked, exhausted and coated in evil-smelling, thick, glutinous mud. Martin Coysh, the young camper, cleaned her up and looked after her for the night. Local boatmen with a lifetime's experience of the river assume that she let herself be carried by the tide in mid-channel, which was then flowing at about $3\frac{1}{2}$ knots, and came ashore probably assisted by a back eddy. They considered she had had a miraculous escape, and that had she panicked or been less resolute she could never have lived. Midge, true to the tenacity typical of her breed, was not put off by her experience and remained as fond of the water as ever.

Some months later there was a big effort to get a large dog fox that had been killing lambs a few miles away. He had gone to earth and though terriers had been put on to bolt him out so that he could be shot they, with the sixth sense most terriers have, showed unusual restraint. Then Midge, the sailor, several times a grandmother, weight 12lb, height 11in, arrived. Without the slightest hesitation in she went. Time passed with no sign of her, and so Mr Pyatt started to dig. It was a long job, for the lair was some 12ft below the ground and about 25ft from the entrance. As Mr Pyatt dug down, so he began to smell a particular kind of poison and knew that somebody had been there before them, and in a hurry for results. Eventually he came upon Midge, still on her feet and still facing inwards, game to the last despite the gas which had crept up on her and stilled the brave little heart. They buried her beneath a large tree, and all who had known her thought the least they could do was to mark the spot. So a

E

brass plaque there commemorates a courageous little dog. It reads:

> Beneath this tree lies Midge
> A little terrier with a big heart
> Killed below ground, December 1970

Her progeny lives on. Nettel, one of her grand-daughters is also mad about boats, but she will never make another Midge—her sort do not come often.

PRIMO SAVED HIS MASTER

Mr Leslie Dennis of Hull is a bachelor and his constant companion was Primo, a four-year-old black, tan and cream alsatian. Whether his master went walking, driving or sailing, Primo was there as a matter of course.

One Easter they went to Scotland for a holiday and Mr Dennis decided that he would climb Britain's highest mountain, Ben Nevis, which rises to 4,406ft. So with Primo he set off one morning at nine, and though there was some snow on the ground and visibility was not very good, all went well and they reached the summit by mid-afternoon. On the descent, however, it started to snow and the track was soon obliterated. So Primo was put on a leash and given his head. There was no question about what he had to do—he simply took the lead and sniffed out the track. The snow became worse and a blizzard developed but Primo did not falter. Under almost impossible conditions the dog led the way back to the hotel, undoubtedly saving his master's life.

Some months later Mr Dennis went sailing on the river Humber, and was to take part in the first race of the season. As Primo had once before been frightened at the sound of the starting gun, Mr Dennis checked with the committee that they would not be using the gun on this occasion. They were alongside a pontoon waiting for the starting signal and suddenly the ten-minute gun was fired. Just as suddenly, Primo leapt for the pontoon and was off. Nobody worried unduly, for this had also happened before and they expected that he would run along the foreshore and then come back as he had done the previous year. An hour later Mr Dennis returned but there was no sign of Primo.

It was later ascertained that he had run along the foreshore to a sheep farm, so Mr Dennis began a search that lasted for many weeks. He enlisted the help of schoolchildren, local police and farmers, offering £100 reward for any news of the dog, but all to no avail. At length he had to accept the fact that Primo would never be seen again. There are strong indications that he was shot as a stray, but there is no proof.

SOUTH AFRICA, HERE WE COME!

When the Dubery family decided to emigrate to South Africa, it was emigration with a vengeance, for accompanying them were two veteran horses saved from the slaughterhouse, three cats, a pekinese and a canary. Certainly Mr and Mrs Dubery, who formerly lived in Sussex, had their worries, but they also got a lot of fun out of mounting their expedition—for it was nothing less than that.

The story started some five years before, when they heard that three elderly ladies living near them had organised a 'Save the Irish horses' fund and were buying old horses destined for the Irish slaughterhouses and bringing them back to end their days in peace and plenty. Like many other people, they found the idea of killing off retired horses for meat repugnant to them, but these three ladies had made an effort to do something about it. Among the rescued were an aged cart horse and a permanently lame riding horse, and these two the Duberys offered to take off their hands and look after.

As the time for emigration approached Mr and Mrs Dubery

realised the terrible wrench it was going to be to leave the horses and their other pets behind. Finally, they made enquiries and found that at some sacrifice, and at a cost of £800 ($2,000), all their livestock could accompany them on the 6,000 mile trip to South Africa. Paperwork is no less for emigrating animals than for humans, so there were import and currency permits to be obtained from South Africa and sworn declarations, veterinary surgeons' certificates and so on, from Britain.

The fun began when they were awaiting the arrival of the horses for loading on to the ship at Southampton. A gang of dockers showed more than usual interest in the detailed arrangements and, thinking that all the fuss heralded a famous racehorse at least, approached Mr Dubery for a racing tip. When he declined they felt he was a mean so-and-so and showed it. But when the horses arrived and Bill, the dear old carthorse, ambled out they just could not believe their eyes. Getting the horse into the spacious box provided was a difficult operation, until the Duberys held a rope across his hind legs to overcome his reluctance. This gave rise to a comment from a docker, 'Just like all the ladies, tickle their legs and they'll do anything'. The roar of laughter which followed made co-operation in the loading a joy.

On board, the horseboxes were placed behind a glass screen on the sports deck and Bill and Bridie quickly became firm favourites of passengers and crew alike. The animals must have felt like film stars. Apples and sugar were lavished upon them: the steward at the Dubery's table could not for a long time understand why he had to be continually replenishing the sugar bowl. On arrival, the older horse had put on so much weight that he could only just get out of the box.

The cats Tom, Tim and Tiny shared a spare cabin with the pekinese and the canary. They kept catching cold, and due to the motion of the ship the antibiotics they were dosed with more often than not ended up as a gooey mess on their fur. But they too survived the voyage and on arrival went into quarantine with the rest of the animals for a three-week period, after which they joined Mr and Mrs Dubery outside Durban, and began their new life in a strange country.

The horses have achieved an even higher standard of life than they enjoyed in Sussex, for they are hosed down by a boy every morning. The cats perhaps, have had more to put up with, and have had to learn the technique of dealing with ticks. Cats, however, can be safely trusted to cope with all situations as they arise.

And as for the humans, Mr and Mrs Dubery feel it was all worth while a thousand times over.

ANNABEL—A REAL PIN-UP

One day a New Forest farmer reported to Mrs Margaret Passmore that a very young jenny donkey foal she owned gave every indication of having a severely injured leg. The foal, Annabel, was just five weeks old, so she was collected and taken back to the farm where it was seen that one hind leg swung about in an ominous manner. She was loaded into the station wagon and driven to the vet, a proceeding that gave following motorists just another proof that when it comes to animals the British are quite mad. After all, who would expect a tiny donkey to be taken for a ride in a car!

At the surgery Annabel was perfectly happy under sedation and fell asleep on the operating table while the X-ray plates were developed. Those concerned realised then that a five-week-old donkey has the same capacity as a twenty-year-old when it comes to snoring. The X-ray showed a fractured femur and all were saddened by the thought that the foal's days were over, when the vet suggested he might be able to operate. A few hours later, the owner heard by telephone that the operation had been successful and that the animal could be collected next day. All night long the foal's mother, disturbed at the loss of her youngster, brayed like a liner at sea in a fog. The racket went on and on without respite, and she was in particularly good voice between the hours of 2 and 4 am.

When they went to collect her next day, Annabel looked really pathetic. Her completely shorn flank revealed a 10in cut sewn with a dozen stitches, and, protruding from it, the end of a 9in stainless steel pin. After the commotion in the night, one would like to think that the reunion between mother and daughter was spectacular. It was not. Annabel made straight for the 'milk bar' and drank long and with obvious satisfaction.

After an uncomfortable week, she began to enjoy her convalescence on a special section of the lawn. Five weeks later the pin was removed and Annabel now has the distinction of being, as far as we know, the only donkey that has ever had a fractured leg steel-pinned.

Now she is as full of beans as any other young donkey and of course a firm favourite, not only with the family but with all the youngsters who live nearby.

OLD BILL THE BENEVOLENT VETERAN

He was named Billy, but over the years has become Old Bill to everyone. The appellation fits him, for in human terms he has clocked up no fewer than 107 years and is still going strong. Even in animal terms, having just passed his forty-third birthday he is a real veteran and bids fair to qualify for inclusion in the *Guinness Book of Records* as the oldest living pony. As far as is known the nearest competitor for the title is a French pony who is believed to be fifty-four, but his claims are not so well authenticated as are those of Old Bill.

A Dartmoor pony, he was purchased at a sale and given to Mrs A. Hall thirty years ago as a present from her father on her sixth birthday. He has been with the family ever since. In his younger days Bill disliked being caught, and used to run at his mistress with mouth wide open and teeth bared; and he always tried all door and gate catches to see if he could break through to the feed store. But together they won literally hundreds of prizes at gymkhanas and pony clubs, and in fact they never competed without winning a prize of some kind.

Old Bill remained with her when she married and since then her three children, now aged fourteen, ten and four, have all learned to ride on him.

Twice in his long life Old Bill has been at death's door, but the care and attention showered on him brought him back to full health. Indeed, until a year ago Mrs Hall's father used him to go round the farm inspecting the cattle and sheep. But now, apart from giving rides to some of the small tots in the neighbourhood, working days are over.

What pleasure he has given in his long life to so many, and may he live on for a long time yet!

THE HORSE THAT DISAPPEARED

One of the saddest stories about a girl and her horse concerns fifteen-year-old Jennifer Dickinson and Ginny, a roan mare. Ginny was a gift to Jennifer from her parents, who had paid 100 guineas for the animal, and it was a gift that gave her tremendous pleasure. Every day for four years she groomed, fed and rode Ginny, but one morning when she arrived at the field where the horse grazed, it was not to be seen.

Jennifer and her parents immediately reported their loss, and a search was begun that went on for weeks. In the end they arrived at a probable explanation of Ginny's disappearance, but this was cold comfort to Jennifer, for her mare has never been traced. It was the custom of the police to use the field in which Ginny grazed as a pound for stray horses while an effort was made to trace their owners. One day a grey mare was found wandering and she was put in the field, but when after three months no owner had come forward to claim her arrangements were made to sell the mare by auction, which was the normal procedure for unclaimed strays. It seems very likely that the owner saw the notice of auction, went to the field beforehand and, without informing anyone, took his horse away. The next day the police arrived to collect the mare and, finding only Ginny in the field, assumed this was the grey they were looking for, and took her off to the sale.

When Jennifer discovered her loss she immediately reported the case and circumstances, but although urgent enquiries were made, it was too late. And sold Ginny must have been, but as is often the way at horse sales, she changed hands so rapidly that it was impossible to trace the last owner. The police set up a local inquiry and the help of a daily newspaper was invoked, but no news came of the missing horse.

Naturally Jennifer was inconsolable, as anyone who has had a close association with an animal over a long period will appreciate. Compensation was of course paid but one cannot replace a friend so easily—and there is always a nagging worry at the back of Jennifer's mind about what exactly did happen to her beloved Ginny.

HELP AT HAND

TRAMPUS FINDS A NEW HOME

When rabies struck the Camberley district of Surrey in October 1969, there were all sorts of minor tragedies. Sad to say, many people panicked and deliberately turned their pets astray with the result that the police found many wandering, both hungry and bewildered. One of these was a mongrel-type terrier bitch about five months old, who was dubbed Trampus. As no one claimed her within seven days she was due to be destroyed.

The National Canine Defence League stepped in, however, and together with four other dogs, Trampus was placed with Miss M. A. Whittock of Palex Kennels, Sussex. Her companions were all dogs of breeding and when some months later they were free to leave the kennels, homes were easily found for them. But Trampus was only a mongrel and did not seem to have any friends at all. Long after the quarantine restrictions were lifted she remained, for Miss Whittock found her an appealing little animal.

As a result of a picture and a short story in the *Sunday Express* scores of others felt as Miss Whittock did, and offers to give her a home poured in. The telephone at the kennels did not stop ringing for three days. Eventually Trampus was placed with Mr and Mrs Tomlinson of Harrow, who had recently lost a boxer which had been with them for thirteen and a half years. Trampus quickly settled down and whilst nervous of people at first, she soon lost her fears. Other dogs she loves, and regardless of colour or size, will dash across the park to make their acquaintance.

On 7 September 1970, 85 dogs and 150 cats were joyfully reclaimed by their owners from quarantine kennels after nine months' enforced separation caused by the rabies scare. Three weeks later, a further 1,100 dogs and 200 cats which had not completed nine months' quarantine were released after being twice vaccinated.

NEW LIFE FOR NODDY

Noddy, a four-year-old pony, is another very lucky animal. After an operation, the first of its kind ever attempted on an animal, he is back as a playmate companion to four-year-old Helen Evans.

The pony was purchased by Mr W. Evans of Leighton Buzzard in Bedfordshire for his granddaughter, but after a while he was disturbed to find that Noddy always seemed to be gasping for breath. He therefore arranged for him to be taken to the Equine Research Centre at Newmarket where it was discovered that the pony had sustained an injury some time before as a result of which its windpipe had become severely restricted. The immediate verdict was that Noddy would have to be destroyed. There was just a chance, however, that if an operation could be performed successfully then the pony might be brought back to full health.

The vet undertook the operation in conjunction with a leading surgeon, and they followed the technique used on human patients of inserting a hollow polythene tube to keep the damaged tissues in place. The tube remained in position for four months and when it was removed the windpipe was found to be completely repaired. It was a case of satisfaction all round, but the delight of Helen in having her playmate back knew no bounds.

An unusual member of the staff at the Equine Research Centre is Honey, a three-year-old Irish wolfhound. He is the resident blood donor, and can give up to two pints without any difficulty at all. When HRH Princess Anne officially opened the hospital for small animals at the centre some time ago, Honey was high on the introduction list.

The Equine Research Centre is one of the research institutes of the Animal Health Trust, an independent organisation devoted to the study of domesticated animals in health and disease and of improvement of veterinary education. The facilities at Newmarket include one of the best operating theatres for animals in the world, and the centre aims to improve the general standard of health of all horses and ponies. The Horserace Betting Levy Board donates £50,000 ($130,000) per annum towards this work, but for the rest the station relies on voluntary contributions from all who love and get pleasure from horses and ponies.

CAT FALLS EIGHTEEN STOREYS AND LIVES

In the heart of traffic-ridden New York City is a very busy and beautifully equipped hospital, with fourteen doctors and surgeons, an outpatients' clinic and X-ray room, and wards that can take 180 in-patients. There is just one great difference from the normal hospital: it has cages in its wards instead of beds, for it is run exclusively for animals. During any year an average of 38,000 animals are treated, the pets of rich and poor alike. An amazing range of both animals and injuries are catalogued in the day-to-day running of the establishment. It is no wonder staff have ceased to be surprised by anything.

Dogs, cats, rabbits, parakeets, monkeys are all of course expected. There are also ocelots and turtles, and other exotic
pets. A 300lb pig which had been savagely attacked by dogs,
and a 7ft boa constrictor, 6in thick, are among the more unusual cases treated. As it is illegal to keep snakes in New York,
this one was sent to a zoo. The pig was a friendly creature,
rejoicing in the name of Arnold, and gave children rides on
his back. There was also a lion which had swallowed a belt
buckle. That was retrieved successfully, and all in the daily
round of the Henry Bergh Memorial Hospital of the American Society for the Prevention of Cruelty to Animals—
founded in 1912 and situated on 92nd Street, Manhattan.

In New York more than 5,000 of the city's canine population of 307,000 are injured by cars each year, all because
owners allow their dogs to run free of the leash. In itself this
is a hazard, but is also a breach of the law. The New York City
Health Code requires that dogs in public places must be re-
strained by a leash no longer than 6ft. This applies in city
streets or parks. Non-observance is punishable by a fine of up
to 25 dollars or imprisonment for ten days, or both. Some cats
also are involved in incidents with cars, but the highest rate
of injuries to the felines is nearly always caused by falling
out of windows. The most remarkable was perhaps the cat
that fell eighteen storeys. It suffered two broken legs and an
injured lung but lived. The staff believe it to have been the
longest fall for an animal to survive.

Perhaps one of the strangest cases the ASPCA has handled
in recent years resulted from a 2 am call at the end of one
summer, reporting that hundreds of migrating birds were
crashing into the Empire State building which rises 1,250ft
in the sky. Most of the birds were killed instantly, but some
still alive were collected and cared for, though very few ulti-
mately survived. The birds were of some twenty different
species, including even thrushes.

Why they flew into the building remains an unsolved mystery, for normally they fly at 1,500 to 3,000ft. A theory put

forward by ornithologists is that the flocks became confused by the changing front and dazzling lights of the building that showed through the low cloud cover over New York that night. Something in the haze puzzled the birds and those that did not crash into the building were probably bewildered and circled it until they were exhausted. The recurrence of such a catastrophe is unlikely as the Empire State building now has its powerful floodlights turned off during spring and summer migrations.

So the great work of the ASPCA goes on, 2,400 major operations being performed each year, from the setting of fractures and tumour removal to heart surgery and even cancer treatment. A $10,000 grant was given by the New York Cancer Research Institute to help in the work at the Henry Bergh Memorial Hospital. This seems a more humane and sensible way of forwarding cancer research than thousands of experiments on animals which are alive and well.

COSTERMONGER'S PONY STARTS A LIFE'S WORK

Visitors to the south and west of England are always delighted to see the wild ponies roaming at will in the New Forest or over Exmoor and Dartmoor.

The moor ponies are owned by the local farmers and each year, at the end of the summer, there is a 'pony gathering' when they are rounded up in order that the 'suckers' or colts born during the year can be marked by the owners of the mares with which they are running. The youngsters are usually sent back to the moor until they are two or three years old and then, after three years of glorious freedom, they are again collected for the pony fair, where dealers from all parts of the country come to buy.

In the New Forest there are some 3,000 adult ponies, plus the youngsters, running free, and all are owned by 'commoners' who live within the Forest boundaries and possess a minimum of one acre of land. The round-ups in the Forest (known as 'drifts') take place a little earlier than those on the moors, and six sales are held every year.

Despite the charming picture they make, it is very wrong for visitors to feed these animals for it attracts them away from the remote parts of the forest or moor to the roads, where at least two a week are killed by traffic. They do not need the food and the offerings of visitors make them spoiled and often vicious.

It is sad to think of these wild ponies, which have enjoyed two or three years of complete freedom, being rounded up and brought into the pens, surrounded by noise and bustle which is completely foreign to them; sadder still when they are purchased by unscrupulous dealers who transport them, often over long distances, to resell. Although the RSPCA and kindred societies are always on the look-out, the ponies sometimes travel without food or water, and often the load includes ponies which are sick or have been injured in the *mêlée* of the sales. Two years ago new government regulations were brought in prohibiting the export of ponies valued at under £70 ($180). This is certainly an improvement but like most Acts still has loopholes for the unscrupulous. One result of the regulations has been to increase the number of scrub ponies auctioned in Britain because the cheaper ponies cannot now be exported.

Mr and Mrs P. Hunt, who run the Home of Rest for horses at Bransby in Lincolnshire are specially concerned about the plight of some of these ponies. The home is situated some thirty miles from Mansfield, which is in the very centre of the working-horse trade in Britain and where every fortnight more than 100 ponies and horses are sold, in addition to those that exchange hands at the two annual fairs.

Every year thousands of unbroken ponies are purchased at the sales on Dartmoor, Exmoor, in the New Forest and in Wales by dealers who resell them all over Britain and Northern Ireland. Many of these animals, Mr Hunt asserts, should never have left their native breeding grounds either on account of age or general fitness. The size of the traffic in native ponies may be estimated from the fact that in one week alone in 1969-70 one dealer bought 500 foals from Dartmoor and Wales.

Mr Hunt attends many of the sales on his errands of mercy and recently was able to snatch a batch of six ponies from death's door. They cost him £100 ($260). They were in a pitiable condition; one had been starved, another was completely blind and also terribly thin, a third staggered round on three legs—one leg having been badly broken at some time and left untreated. One poor little Welsh colt had a permanently deformed face, its top jaw being inches out of line with its lower jaw, and because it could not chew properly had been cruelly neglected. Another, and probably the most pathetic of the six, was a Dartmoor colt covered in deep weals and unhealed scars caused by severe beatings. The mystery is why people buy ponies in this condition, but obviously they find a market somewhere.

Mr Hunt was emphatic that although he had been rescuing horses for twenty-three years, these were the worst cases of cruelty he had seen. They were all taken to the Home, and all were nursed back to health. But this is more than one man's work, and Mr Hunt has protested to the Ministry of Agriculture, urging that more supervision should be given at sales by Ministry veterinary surgeons.

Mr Hunt started on this work when, as a young lad, he became acquainted with a skewbald mare which pulled a costermonger's cart round the streets of London selling logs. The animal had obviously been put to work at a very early age and although only four years old was already worn out. Her owner stabled her in a furniture van and one night during a storm she broke loose and was found wandering with a car tyre round her neck. Mr Hunt bought her for £14 ($35) and that was the beginning of his plan for a sanctuary for horses.

Sally, this first pony, is still with them. At least some recompense has been made for her for the suffering of her early years. Now twenty-six, she still enjoys life with the others at the Home.

Pledged to the protection of the native moorland ponies and the provision of a sanctuary for old working horses, all the work of the establishment is voluntary. When an animal is fit enough, it can be placed in a home under agreement, but none of the rescued are ever sold. Those that, on humanitarian grounds, cannot be kept alive are put down on the premises under veterinary supervision.

There are some 10 acres of rich grazing land where the animals can roam and today there are about twenty of them, numbers being restricted only by the amount of money available.

THE STREET OF THE ENGLISH LADY

Sikket el Sitt Inglisia—so the poor of Cairo call the street where the Brooke Hospital for Animals is situated. Meaning literally 'street of the English lady', it is a perpetual monument to the memory of a great lady, Mrs Geoffrey Brooke.

The story goes back to the end of the first world war and a British government faced with the problem of getting the allied soldiers home at a time when there was an acute shortage of ships. It was decided that the 22,000 cavalry horses in the Middle East could not be repatriated and should be sold off. In 1930 Mrs Brooke, the wife of Major General G. F. H. Brooke who commanded a cavalry brigade, arrived in Egypt and saw with horror again and again that fine old horses bearing the brand of the British Army were being maltreated or overworked. Straining at heavy loads, falling exhausted under the lash, many more than half-starved—this

Page 93   The dolphin's power of propulsion is enormous (page 100)

Page 94 Dignified magnificence, Shire horses on show (page 113)

was the lot of the fine animals that deserved better of a victorious nation—particularly a nation of animal lovers. Naturally the horses were much prized by their new masters for their strength and stamina, but by the time Mrs Brooke arrived in Cairo only the very strongest had survived the heat, the flies and, in so many cases, the ill-treatment.

Many other expatriates were probably appalled at the fate of the cavalry horses in Egypt, but Mrs Brooke decided to do something about it. So she set herself the task of buying up such horses as had survived their servitude, and when she appealed in English newspapers for donations to enable her to undertake an Old War Horse Rescue Campaign, there was a generous response. Then she let it be known that she was willing to purchase the veteran horses. For three years a steady stream of them were brought to her; most of them were broken and suffering and had to be painlessly destroyed. But in three heart-rending years Mrs Brooke achieved her aim. In that time she had traced and bought nearly 5,000 horses, all that remained of the original number that had been sold in Egypt.

Most people perhaps would have rested content at that, but Mrs Brooke, during her crusade in Egypt, had come to realise the plight of the native-born horses, mules and donkeys. So in 1934 she set up a permanent Old War Horse Memorial Hospital, providing skilled veterinary attention for all animals, a service that was free to the often poverty-stricken owners. Every penny, first for the hospital and then for its upkeep, was raised by Mrs Brooke herself, right up to the time of her death in Cairo in 1955.

So this humane and philanthropic work has gone on. Its purpose is twofold: first to provide treatment for suffering animals: secondly, and even more important, to encourage local inhabitants to accept the responsibility of caring for their own animals.

It is essential that animals are taken to the hospital voluntarily, for any form of compulsion would only encourage an

F

ignorant owner to hide his sick beast or work him under cover of darkness, or worse still let him die uncared for. The hospital and its staff have had a long uphill fight against poverty, superstition, apathy and ignorance, but considerable progress has been made over the years. Many of the very poor Egyptian families do in fact look after their animals, as far as is in their power, but it must be remembered that life is also very hard and difficult for them, and where the animal is their only means of livelihood they try to keep the beast going whatever its condition.

The hazards of life in the East, even for an animal that has been well-cared for, are formidable. The greatest proportion of the cases treated at the hospital result from accidents on the overcrowded roads. Then comes general weakness due largely to overwork and possibly underfeeding as well, and third in the list comes lameness, usually a result of overloading.

In addition to the work at the hospital in Cairo, veterinary surgeons attend a number of weekly markets on the look-out for animals needing treatment. In an average year these alone total well over 6,000. And in addition to all this, some 600 animals yearly are purchased in order to put them humanely out of their misery. There are many other facets to the work, including the erection of drinking troughs and shelters wherever the need is seen to be great.

Mrs Brooke kept a diary of her early work (now published in book form, *For Love of Horses*). It tells not only of the almost insuperable difficulties she had to contend with but also of some fascinating and heart-warming episodes. Since Mrs Brooke's death, Mrs Kathleen Taylor Smith has been Honorary Organiser and Treasurer of the Memorial hospital. The work continues to expand, and veterinary clinics have now been opened in Alexandria and Luxor, Upper Egypt. It still rests entirely on the generosity of private individuals and is a fine example of the humane work for animals which has so often emanated from Britain.

A FITTING MEMORIAL

Speaking in the House of Lords in 1957, Air Chief Marshal Lord Dowding put his views on the animal world in this way:

> The animals are our younger brothers and sisters. This is an important part of our responsibilities to help them, and not to retard their development by cruel exploitation of their helplessness.
>
> Failure to recognise our responsibilities to the animal kingdom is the cause of many of the calamities which now beset the nations of the world. We shall never attain to true peace until we recognise the place of animals in the scheme of things, and treat them accordingly.

When he died in 1970, large numbers of people in all walks of life urged that he should be suitably commemorated, for he was largely responsible for the successful outcome of the Battle of Britain.

Donations began to flow in and Lady Dowding consulted friends and former colleagues of the Air Marshal as to what form a memorial could take. As a result, a charitable trust —the Dowding Sanctuary—was established. Few animal lovers would disagree with the terms set out:

> The establishment of an animal sanctuary as the lasting memorial to the late Air Chief Marshal Lord Dowding, GCB, GCVO, CMG, and in commemoration of his victory of the Battle of Britain under his leadership.
>
> To relieve animals, both wild and domesticated, from distress; to prevent cruelty to such animals. To conserve and care for animals in their natural habitat.
>
> As a result of research to educate public opinion to a greater awareness of the special problems which affect animal welfare arising from urbanisation, pollution of the atmosphere, and the use of chemical sprays.

So the plans are laid. It is intended to purchase a property in Kent or Sussex (the main Battle of Britain area) and on it establish wildlife reservations; no chemical sprays or fertilisers will be used on the grounds it is hoped that some of the birds and butterflies which have long since disappeared from the countryside will return. A refuge is to be provided for abandoned animals, and none will be put to sleep unless this is found to be absolutely necessary. The trustees hope that there will be fields where old horses can live out their lives.

Bearing in mind the character of the man after whom the sanctuary is named, how much more fitting and sensible a memorial this will be than a bronze statue.

DOG-CATCHER—TWENTIETH CENTURY

In the eighteenth century churchwardens regularly appointed a dog-catcher to deal with dogs in churches. Now in the twentieth century it has become necessary, for entirely different reasons, for some cities to appoint official dog-catchers. One of the first to do so was Bristol, where stray dogs had become something of an embarrassment and a definite traffic hazard. In one year a total of 1,212 stray dogs were seized by the police, and of these only 204 could be immediately restored to their owners, 21 were retained by the finders and 987 were sent to the Bristol Dogs Home from where 441 were eventually claimed by their owners, 117 were sold and the remaining 429 destroyed.

In April 1970 the City Council issued an order (Control of Dogs on Roads), making it an offence to allow any dog to stray on public highways within the city. To enforce the order a dog warden was appointed. His job is to conduct daily patrols with a motor van, to collect any dogs found straying and to take them first to a police station for registration and then to a dogs' home. During his first year of operation he collected some 218 dogs, included in the overall figure above, and 34 dog owners were convicted for offences contrary to the order. Between January and May of 1971,

103 dogs were collected by the warden.

All this makes sad reading, particularly as the owners are at fault and the animals suffer for it. Even more important is the fact that stray dogs are such a major traffic hazard. It is very necessary that the public should be taught to maintain proper control over their dogs and it is hoped that the appointment of the warden will awaken people to a sense of their responsibilities.

Scunthorpe in Lincolnshire is one of the great steel towns of Europe and, strange to say, this was the primary reason for the appointment of a dog-catcher there. Strays in general were, of course, a danger in traffic, as they are everywhere, but dogs causing most concern in Scunthorpe belonged to men who were in the habit of coming home from a late shift at the steel mills, letting the dog out and then promptly forgetting about it. Off went the dog with his cronies and before long a pack had gathered and fights and chaos ensued.

A bylaw of the borough made it an offence for an owner to walk a dog in the town without a collar—complete with identity disc—and a lead, a law which was obeyed by most people. Nevertheless, a great many dogs still ran loose and so it was decided to appoint a dog-catcher or canine control officer to pick up any dog found running free. Miss Barbara O'Connor, whose parents own kennels in the town, was the successful applicant and so became Britain's first woman dog-catcher. In the first twelve months some 300 dogs (80 per cent of them without identity discs) were collected and over half were claimed by their owners. Of those remaining, about 70 per cent were found new homes and the others had to be destroyed at the RSPCA clinic.

The amazing thing is that most of the animals are well-fed and in good condition when they are picked up. Most are mongrels but there are also labradors, alsatians, Jack Russells and the like among the unclaimed strays. Those with a name-tag are, of course, taken to their owners with a caution. Most owners are grateful, but some are offensive, and naturally any girl doing such a job is a target for strong feelings.

One day she discovered a mongrel tied to a lamp post and having waited around for a time eventually took the dog in. After ten days it was destroyed and then a man went to the police enquiring for his lost 'alsatian'. He maintained he left it tied to a lamp post while he just popped into the betting shop!

Quite often puppies of six to eight weeks are among the strays. This is usually because people have not bothered to train them, and so when they foul a carpet or try their teeth on a table leg, they are just thrown out. Often a child has a puppy as a present but when the novelty wears off the poor animal receives no more consideration than last year's Christmas tree and is soon disowned.

Many so-called guard dogs also get a raw deal. They are chained up all day or night, or locked in a small back yard while the family is out at work all day. They naturally get bad-tempered and often vicious. Miss O'Connor has been able to make something of some she has recovered, but the majority have to be destroyed. It was one of these frustrated guard dogs that made his mark on her hand, and several stitches were necessary. Fortunately, occurrences such as this are rare.

With all its trials and tribulations Miss O'Connor loves the work and feels she is making a worthwhile contribution to road safety and to animal welfare. She has also found time to marry and become Mrs Hiscock.

A MEASURE OF FREEDOM

AFRICA IN WINDSOR

In the last few years there has been a considerable increase in the number of wild life and safari parks, where wild animals can roam in extensive reserves, in as near natural conditions as possible. It would seem that this is a tremendous advance on the ordinary zoo, where so often animals are penned into barred and wired cages with concrete floors, and where only very restricted movement is possible.

One of the most popular and largest of such parks in England is the Royal Windsor Safari Park in Berkshire, visited by a million or more people each year. It was opened in 1970 by a company formed from members of the Smart family, famous in the entertainment and circus world and with long experience in working with animals. The reserve covers some 150 acres and at present is the home of some 200 species, their numbers continually increasing. From the outset the company aimed to give the maximum freedom possible to the larger animals, a concession that called for maximum security. This is certainly first class; the park is compact and no one is ever out of sight of the patrol cars.

One of the chief justifications for zoos has always been that they serve the purpose of preserving and continuing species that are fast dying out. But it has also been established that natural conditions are more conducive to breeding, so the wild life parks obviously have a great advantage here. Certainly some considerable successes have been achieved. Recently a record was set up when quins were born to a lioness in captivity; and at Windsor the park authorities were delighted when, not so long ago, a llama produced offspring in the summer whereas before births had always been in the winter. These and similar cases suggest that the animals must be content in their surroundings.

Animals, with few exceptions, all tend to live longer in captivity—if conditions are good—than they do in the wild state. Lions, for instance, have a life expectancy of fourteen or fifteen years in the wild, but in captivity they can live to twenty-five or more. Lionesses, however, do not usually make good mothers in captivity, even in the best conditions, and without supervision few of their cubs would survive. At Windsor one lion cub was fostered out to Sheana, an alsatian bitch of two and a half years, and a fine job she made of rearing both her pups and the stranger in their midst.

A lion in the wild has its own natural territory which borders on but does not overlap that of its neighbours. In order to keep this delicate balance of power lions have to know each other, and before they are released into their enclosures at Windsor they are mingled together so that they can form associations and become members of a pride where none is a stranger.

These lions are in two enclosures: a younger group of two- to three-year-olds, and those that are mature. In all there are sixty of them. Napoleon and Josephine are brother and sister, and at two years they weigh over 300lb. In maturity the beasts measure up to 10ft from nose to tail and can weigh anything up to 450lb. The cheetahs, too, have a reserve but this member of the cat family is considered a meaner fellow. This swiftest of all animals is built like a greyhound and in its native environment is reputed to attain speeds of up to seventy miles an hour.

The large baboon reserve contains some 180 animals and includes all ages from new-born babies to fully grown monkeys of eight years. They run quite free, but the dominant male will often kill the young if not prevented. If you watch them as visitors drive through, you realise what a keen intelligence and sense of fun these creatures have. They have quickly come to terms with the motor-car and take a jump on to a moving vehicle just for the ride, their nimble fingers exploring all accessible parts and components. The keepers are devoted to their charges, one of them says he would sooner spend all day with 180 baboons than 180 humans: they are not so stupid.

Much trouble is caused in zoos and parks by visitors who persist in feeding the animals, most of which are much better off on the regular diet provided by their keepers. There was considerable concern at Windsor recently when one of the young Indian elephants was taken ill and it was discovered that he had swallowed a plastic bag. He finally recovered but a keeper sat up with him night after night for a fortnight. Had the bag entered the wrong way round, nothing could have saved him. As it was five hundred tins of creamed rice, a daily ration of six bottles of Ribena, and the constant attention of the keeper got him back to health.

The elephant, like the whale, lives to about sixty years. Their appetites seem to be on a par too. The former consumes several hundred pounds of food and thirty to fifty gallons of water each day: the whale gets through some 250lb of fish. The latest addition to the Safari Park is a young killer whale, 14ft long and weighing some 1,500lb. When fully grown in about ten years time it will weigh more than 5 tons and measure 30ft or so. This amazing animal has quickly responded to training and has been taught to obey commands by the whistle. His diet is mainly herring and mackerel; at present he gets through 50lb a day but as he grows this will no doubt rise to the expected 250lb. Many are the arguments over the assessment of animal intelligence relative to that of man, but scientists are agreed that the whale family, including porpoises and dolphins, scores best among animals and comes not so very far behind humans. One assessment gives relative brain power in the following terms: fish less than 1, horse 2.5, cat 4 or 5, ape 8, porpoise 36, man 50. The largest brain ever found was in a sperm whale: it weighed 19lb.

The high intelligence of dolphins, one of the smaller members of the whale family, and their ability to learn, has brought the animal into prominence in recent years. Unfortunately in many places dolphins are shown without a real understanding of their needs and health, and this must take a real toll of the species. Dolphins are, of course, mammals, warm-blooded animals giving milk and breathing air, and are to be found in almost every ocean in the world though most are caught off the coast of Florida or California. There are probably sixty different species, but the average dolphin is about 5ft 10in long and weighs up to 300lb.

In their wild state they keep to well-defined territories of about 100 square miles. Led usually by a bull, they wander in groups combing the ocean for food. The whistle or sound that they emit from a hole in the top of the head can be heard and recognised by others of the species for a distance of twenty miles under water. They never seem to sleep in the accepted sense, but rest in a semi-torpid state in the water, rarely closing both eyes. It surprises many people to learn that dolphins must have air. If they were to be kept under water for ten minutes they would quite possibly burst their lungs.

At Windsor the dolphins are in prime condition; constant attention is paid to their health, including the taking of a blood sample every month. Theirs is the second largest dolphin pool in Britain, containing some 250,000 gallons of 'artificial' sea water which is filtered in at the rate of 60,000 gallons per hour, the temperature being maintained at 65-70°F (18-21°C).

Training of the bottle-nosed dolphin commences as soon as they are able to catch fish, and they soon learn to follow the trainer's whistle which has to be of the correct pitch and tone for the dolphin's hearing. They give every appearance of thoroughly enjoying performing their repertoire: jumping from the water over a line stretched many feet above the pool, manoeuvring a rubber dinghy with a human passenger across the pool, playing forms of water polo and skittles, and jumping through hoops held 10ft above the water. The onlooker is left in no doubt whatever about their very real sense of humour.

Another fascinating animal is the English otter, but it is a sad reflection on Britain that our home species has been so persecuted and hunted that today the English variety has to be imported from India.

PHAROAH FALLS ON HIS FEET

Pharoah is a lion, and no ordinary animal by any standard. His parents, Lucifer and Jenny, were born in South Africa in the Krüger Park, north-east of Johannesburg, but were sent to Britain when in their prime. They settled down well in Lord Gretton's lion reserve at Stapleford Park near Melton Mowbray in Leicestershire, and in due course two male cubs were born. Unfortunately Jenny turned out to be a bad mother and when the warden visited the family the day after they were born, he found one of the cubs already dead. Pharoah, too, had been neglected and there was no time to lose. The pathetic little creature was immediately taken away in a Land Rover, shivering and very weak, and a rescue operation to save his life was mounted immediately. He was put in a box, wrapped in a warm rug and placed in front of a fire pending the arrival of the veterinary surgeon. His verdict was terse: Pharoah was suffering from pneumonia. The cub was at once innoculated but his chances of recovery were rated as poor, everything depending on the utmost care and attention. It was fortunate, therefore, that Mr and Mrs P. Maxwell, who were connected with the lion reserve, were in a position to volunteer to take him into their home and nurse him back to health.

From the beginning it was obvious that Pharoah had a very friendly disposition. He never seemed to resent correction, and when he could have a game with someone—the highlight of his day—he would put on a pretence of boisterousness but went out of his way to be gentle in any rough and tumble.

Gifted with this happy nature, he appeared to like everything else that breathed. On the occasions when he was awkward it was generally because he was getting tired—but he was never bad-tempered and never showed the slightest sign of shooting his claws. He loved to be admired and to be the centre of attraction, and was a natural actor, knowing in some uncanny way exactly what he was required to do, especially when posing for a photograph.

As he grew up Pharoah was taken into the workaday world of human beings and graced the occasion whenever and wherever he went. Often he accompanied Lord Gretton, who had adopted him as a special pet, to speaking engagements. In the car he occupied the back seat and took an interest in everything around him.

When he was a year old he had a special birthday party with the children. He did not think much of the cake—one sniff put him off that—but the flickering candle was really exciting and he could not rest until he had blown it out. He realised that it was his day and that extinguishing the flame was his curtain-call.

Sad to relate Pharoah is now growing up and can no longer be treated as a pet. He will join other lions of his own age group, waiting his turn to go into the reserve and, of course, will later be used for stud purposes. His was an unusual start in life for a lion, but he undoubtedly enjoyed his favoured position and has given tremendous pleasure to many humans.

Stapleford Park lion reserve was founded in 1968 as a

breeding centre, and is now open to the public. It contains between twenty-five and thirty of the finest lions to be seen anywhere in the world.

NOBLE BRITISH BEASTS

BRITAIN'S DEER

One of the most noble of beasts and holding pride of place as the largest of British mammals, is the red deer. In prehistoric days these roamed freely throughout Britain and are still to be found in many places today. It is difficult to give a reliable estimate, but it is generally thought that wild deer of all species in Britain number about 400,000.

A stag grows its first antlers when it is twelve months old. Many people do not realise that antlers are discarded annually, larger new ones growing in the place of the old in approximately the same period of the year as the ferns grow on the hillside. The new growth is protected by a thin skin known as 'velvet', which covers the horn in the growing stage when the slightest knock is liable to cause a deformity, and which, as the horn matures, the stag discards by rubbing against trees. While in the growing stage, the antlers are quite pliable and soft, the velvet being in effect a protection for the blood tissues; when the antler is fully formed the remaining velvet dies off.

The annual transition from the soft velvet to the bone-hard antler is an amazing process, taking about three and a half months to complete, during which time it is essential that the right food and much calcium are available to keep up the spectacular growth rate of 1cm a day. An average red deer lives from twelve to fifteen years, and the antlers are a sign of the age and virility of the stag. As he passes maturity, so he becomes an old man in the herd and is ousted from a position of leadership by a younger stag. By his gait, his dewlap and his big paunch he can easily be spotted by the expert. In his prime a stag may weigh 350lb, his antlers alone being something like 15lb, although heavier sets have been known.

Over the years the red deer in the Lake District have been harried and driven from their natural haunts, a fact which makes it easy for the poacher to corner and shoot them, but Lakeland's Martindale Forest is noted for its ancient herd. They are shy animals, and rarely seen except by those familiar with their movements. Sight, smell and hearing are all acute, the last being probably their most highly developed sense. They can attain a speed of some 35 miles per hour and it is incredible how a stag with a magnificent set of antlers can run in the forest without getting inextricably caught up in trees and bushes. Unfortunately they do occasionally get caught in wire fences.

The red deer in England and Scotland are outnumbered by the roe deer and this animal is possibly the most unusual of all. The buck by marking trees will define his own area and woe betide any rival who trespasses.

In 1953, a number of people formed a group with the object of protecting wild deer in the British Isles, and this later became the British Deer Society. The late Mr Herbert Fooks, a founder-member of the society, who lived at High Hay Bridge, near Bouth, was an authority on deer throughout the world and particularly concerned over the future of Lakeland deer. His widow has now put into effect a project he had long planned, setting aside 200 acres of the most glorious Lakeland country at Hay Bridge as a deer sanctuary. The area comprises moss-land, deciduous woodland and rough grazing, and there are plans to improve the deer habitat by planting more hardwoods and fertilising open grassland.

The numbers of Furness Fell Red, a breed of deer which has retained the character of its primeval ancestors more markedly than any other herd in Britain, have in recent years suffered a sharp decline. One of the aims of High Hay Bridge is to call a halt to this downward trend and ensure the continuance of these magnificent beasts. A small but superb deer museum has been built, primarily to interest the young. There is a splendid display of antlers, pictures of the slots of different types of deer, and provision is to be made for painting, modelling, carving and general study. Out of doors there are plenty of opportunities for the serious study of deer and four high seats have been erected in the reserve specially for viewing them.

The High Hay Bridge Deer Reserve and Museum are not open to the general public, but arrangements can be made with the Education Director for parties of schoolchildren interested in natural history, and for members of naturalists' trusts and natural history societies.

Mrs Fooks has a small enclosure where she keeps three deer, each of which came to her with a 'hard luck story'. The first was a fallow-deer fawn, who arrived at High Hay Bridge when she was a year old and in very bad condition. Now she is flourishing and a mate is being obtained for her. A yearling roebuck came at the tender age of two days, after his mother had become hopelessly entangled in a plastic fence and had to be shot. He was bottle-reared and is remarkably tame. Unfortunately it is in the nature of this breed when they are in hard horn to become dangerous and utterly undependable, and it is necessary to confine them. No matter how docile they may seem, they are never to be trusted.

Mrs Fooks's third acquisition is a most delightful female roe kid. She was apparently dropped by the doe on the main Windermere road and a few minutes later a dog was seen chasing the mother into the woods. The kid was picked up and put on the grass verge, but she was too weak to stand and Mrs Fooks was asked to rear her. That was only the beginning

Page 111 Big Ben and John Bull, magnificent shire horses, welcome an American visitor from Idaho

Page 112 A sad but necessary reminder. Luckily she was saved from a miserable death in East Cornwall. The RSPCA made efforts to find the perpetrator of the deed.

of the story. For the next three weeks she had to be fed at three-hourly intervals day and night. Six weeks elapsed before she was down to a more manageable four feeds a day. But soon she progressed to corn and has grown into a beautiful animal, not a bit shy of humans. These deer come to the call and are a great asset to the general project.

Mrs Fooks has a house imaginatively converted from a sixteenth-century barn, with picture windows that give on to what surely must be one of the finest vistas in Lakeland, and one of the most imaginative and worthwhile projects in conservation and education.

DIGNIFIED MAGNIFICENCE

There are few more beautiful sights than that of a team of magnificent dray horses. Their strength, dignity, uniformity of appearance, their nice nature and shining coats, make them an eye-catcher wherever they appear. The ancestors of this breed were certainly the great war horses of medieval times, strength and stamina then being very necessary when both horse and rider wore armour. Later, they were bred for power in agricultural use and transport generally, the earliest draught stallions coming from Leicestershire, Staffordshire and Derbyshire. Records also show that the Fen country produced a heavy horse which was distributed throughout England.

Over the years every effort has been made to establish uniformity of type, character and appearance and for this purpose the Shire Horse Society was formed in 1878. The shire horse is possessed of all the good qualities looked for in a draught animal—strength, good constitution, stamina, great power and adaptability. With his own great weight, the shire has moved stupendous weights on the most unpropitious terrain. At one London show, weight-pulling tests were arranged to

G

take place on a variety of surfaces, including granite setts. Two shire geldings, yoked tandem fashion, moved off on these wet slippery setts, pulling 18½ tons behind them. When matched against a measuring device at the Wembley Exhibition one year, the maximum pull registered was judged equal to a starting load of 50 tons.

It is little wonder, therefore, that once again these horses are being used by brewery companies for local deliveries of heavy loads in some of our cities. Indeed in Blackburn they have been used continuously since 1807 when they pulled the drays which delivered the first casks of beer brewed by Messrs Daniel Thwaites. Today the firm maintains eight horses of this calibre. Four are used on deliveries within a 1½-mile radius, approximately, and four are used for show purposes, chiefly in the north-west of England. All of them are black shire geldings and cost £350-£400 each when four or five years old. But these are show-team standard, and it is only fair to say that good commercial geldings can be bought for as little as £150 ($390).

The Thwaites' horses each average a ton in weight and it is necessary to have them shod every four to six weeks. They are worked in single harness only, but for show purposes they go in pairs and every endeavour is made to keep each pair together, even to the extent of providing them with adjoining boxes. It has been found that this eliminates any possibility of friction between them. Three weeks every year they have a break from the workaday world and go out to pasture in the Ribble valley.

Recently one of the horses, Drayking, reached retiring age at fourteen years, for ten of which he had served the Company. He was a great favourite, and had achieved some fame apart from the show ring, for he took part in a television programme in the course of which he became England's beer-drinking champion by disposing of five pints in fifty-three seconds! Now he has gone into retirement on a farm near Warrington, where he enjoys his pension of a pint of beer a day.

The present team of eight, rejoicing in the names of Star, William, Mighty, Tiny (weight one ton), Bomber, Royal and James, have won awards all over England, at the Royal Show, the Royal Lancashire, the Cheshire County and a host of others. Perhaps they are best remembered for the splendid spectacle they make at the Wembley Horse of the Year Show, where the team has appeared for eight consecutive years.

On the showground the horses pull 12cwt four-wheel drays painted in red and gold, each dray loaded with three casks, two barrels (36 gallons each), a kilderkin (18 gallons) and crates of bottles. Two kinds of vehicle are used—the Lancashire dray, with an open body, and the London van dray, which has low sides to the body and rear wheels 5ft in diameter. The driver controls his team from a seat 8ft above the ground and has to be strapped to his perch, for a sharp jolt could easily throw him off.

The stable show gear is valued at several hundred pounds. The black leather harness, strengthened in places with steel, is embellished with gleaming brass fittings. A brass star— symbol of the company—shines from the collar, small brass beer casks decorate the blinkers and saddle, and the name of each horse is riveted to the front of his collar. The drivers wear a livery of brown jackets with red facing, cavalry-twill knee breeches, and well-shone brown boots and leggings. Smart grey bowlers and red ties complete the outfits.

But showground work for the horses is simply time off from the daily round. Their normal working day starts at about 7am with a breakfast of bran and chopped hay.

When costs of horse drays and mechanical transport are compared some surprising figures are revealed. The following figures were worked out by Mr David Kay, a past president of the Shire Horse Society. The cost of putting a horse-drawn dray on the road is about £500 ($1,300), £150 ($390) of this for the horse and £350 ($910) for the dray and harness. A motor vehicle to carry a similar load of $2\frac{1}{2}$ tons costs £1,650. A horse purchased at four years old has an average working life of about fourteen years, so depreciation over that period is £500. Lorries, on the other hand, are usually written off over a seven-year period, a depreciation of £3,300 over fourteen years. So that here alone is a definite saving of £2,800.

Taxation on a vehicle suitable for this work would amount to about £85.50. By using a horse instead there would be a further economy of approximately £1,200 over the fourteen-year period. As for running costs, the horse wins handsomely again. Food and veterinary bills per horse per day works out at $36\frac{1}{2}$p. How much for fuel and maintenance of mechanical vehicles! Mr Kay, therefore, asserts that over a fourteen-year period the overall saving is well over £4,000.

Messrs Odnams, a family brewery company of Southwold in Suffolk, used horse transport up to 1953 when their last horse was pensioned off and they went over to motor transport. In 1970, however, they decided to reintroduce horse drays for local deliveries within a five-mile radius, because they reckoned this would be far more economical than continuing with motor lorries at a time when new restrictions and heavy licence duty had put up the cost of transport.

They were fortunate in being able to secure dray horses from another brewery that was being closed down. Among them were two geldings of the famous Percheron Normandy breed of draught horse: John, ten years old, and Bill eighteen but capable of light work. In addition, two four-year-old Shire X Percheron geldings which were trace-broken were purchased for about £200 ($520) each. Their training was finished by Messrs Odnams' own horseman. Also obtained were some working drays and a very fine show dray. The horses quickly settled down in their new surroundings and work a five-day week, the longest round trip they do being about sixteen miles.

WHAT HAPPENED TO THEM

Readers of the first *Book of True Animal Stories* (1970) often write and ask for news about characters that particularly took their fancy. Naturally, I am not able to give up-to-date information on all of them, but here are a few progress reports.

Lucky, the ocean-going goose who was found swimming vigorously twenty miles from land is still doing nicely at the Ingrams' home at Milford Haven. Preferring male company, she has attached herself to Mr Ingram and when she decides to go to bed, comes up from the pool calling at intervals to remind him to fetch her supper. If he is absent for any length of time the reunion is long and vocal. A handsome goose with shrewd blue eyes, she is very much one of the family. Lucky has indeed remained lucky.

Idol, the police alsatian killed when making an arrest, received a posthumous award for his bravery.

Peggy, the mongrel who gave the alarm and saved the lives of Mr and Mrs Warren, both of whom are incapacitated and might have been burnt to death, was also awarded the RSPCA plaque. The terrier is still a guard and treasure to the couple.

Bruce, the labrador hero of the mudflats who saved the life of a four-year-old boy and also received an award, has his real and continuing reward in the adoration of all the children in the neighbourhood. He takes them to school and his 'built-in alarm clock' tells him when it is time to meet them.

In Dunoon, Scotland, Manda, the pet cow, has delivered her fourth calf and her jumping days are over. Nevertheless, she still has a mind of her own. When she suffered a foot injury and could only hobble on three legs, the most stringent precautions had to be taken to ensure she was really locked up for the night, or she would be away with the dairy herd.

Digger, the Australian tough guy, settled down in Margate after all. When his mistress returned to England there was a joyful reunion and now the continent where he was born is but a dim memory.

EPILOGUE

The great work of wildlife conservation is at last under way. The conscience of the world has been prodded and much progress is being made. Twelve Indian states have banned the shooting of tigers because of the alarming fall in their numbers from some 40,000 to fewer than 4,000; sea turtles which were very nearly obliterated because there were no restrictions on the collection of their eggs are now protected; and a whole list of animals has been put on the 'thou shalt not kill' register.

Yet even in western countries—and Britain, for example, is reputed to be a nation of animal lovers—horrifying examples of ignorance and callous cruelty to animals come to light every day. At the Battersea Dogs' Home in London, for instance, 60,000 dogs were brought in as strays in one year, all found within a radius of twenty miles from Charing Cross. Hundreds of other homes are doing the same kind of rescue work. When it is so easy to dispose of an animal in a humane way, or find another home for it, how can one begin to understand people who drop unwanted dogs on a busy motorway, assuming, generally correctly, that they will soon be killed? What kind of man was it who was seen to pull up on a motorway slip road, get out and throw a stick for his dog, and when the animal bounded after it, jump into his car and drive off? Eight hours later the little fellow was picked up, waiting faithfully for the return of his master, and still grasping his stick. Undoubtedly incidents such as these make a strong case for an increased licence fee, which might deter many unsuitable people from taking on a puppy without sufficient thought.

Things are certainly organised more efficiently in New York. Instead of a mere 37½p which is the fee paid in Britain, the licence costs $6.10 (£2.30, roughly). Six dollars are retained by the American Society for the Prevention of Cruelty to Animals, which then has the responsibility of handling lost, stray and unwanted animals, for which purpose the Society maintains five animal centres in the city. The 10 cents go to the state to help finance research into dog diseases and viruses that affect both animals and people. This is not to be confused with vivisection. As a point of interest, almost 3 million dog licences are issued in Great Britain yearly, nearly 300,000 of them in the thirty-two London boroughs. Some 300,000 licences were issued in New York State last year.

It is recorded by the British Home Office that in 1969 13,791 people in Britain were licensed to carry out experiments on animals and 5½ million experiments were in fact carried out, 4¾ million of them without an anaesthetic! It is estimated that one animal dies as a result of these experiments at every second of each working day—a horrifying thought. These things are still governed by the Cruelty to Animals Act of 1876. Add to this the surge forward in factory-farm methods, the latest being battery cages for pigs, and we seriously begin to wonder whether after all the animals are not a higher form of life than the humans who control them.

These macabre facts, figures and developments should pull us up short and make us ponder our attitude to animals and their place in the scheme of things. It is time that we humans, with our supposedly superior brain, should cease to exploit our fellow creatures. We must realise that they are a vital part of our civilisation and recognise their contribution to the evolution of mankind.

ACKNOWLEDGEMENTS

The author gratefully acknowledges help given by the following:

American Society for the Prevention of Cruelty to Animals, 92nd Street, New York, New York 10028

Animal Health Trust (Equine Research Station, Newmarket), 24 Portland Place, London

Brooke Hospital for Animals, Cairo-British Columbia House, 1 Regent Street, London SW1

Dowding Sanctuary Ltd, 1 Calverley Park, Tunbridge Wells, Kent

Home of Rest for Horses, Bransby, Saxilby, Lincolnshire

National Canine Defence League, 10 Seymour Street, London W1H 5WB

Royal Society for the Prevention of Cruelty to Animals, 105 Jermyn Street, London SW1

Shire Horse Society, East of England Showground, Peterborough

The *Sunday Express*, for permission to use the content of two stories: 'Minette' and 'Dog Walks 800 Miles'